If You're Haunted Flaunt It

by

Sharon Saracino

This is a work of fiction. Names, characters, places, and incidents are either the product of the author's imagination or are used fictitiously, and any resemblance to actual persons living or dead, business establishments, events, or locales, is entirely coincidental.

If You're Haunted Flaunt It

Cover Art by *Debbie Taylor*

The Wild Rose Press, Inc.
PO Box 708
Adams Basin, NY 14410-0708
Visit us at www.thewildrosepress.com

Publishing History
First Fantasy Rose Edition, 2016
Print ISBN 978-1-5092-1084-8
Digital ISBN 978-1-5092-1085-5

Published in the United States of America

"Lucy, wake up."

The mattress shook with the ferocity of a magnitude six earthquake. I pressed the pillow more tightly around my head hoping to muffle the intrusive voice.

"C'mon, wakey, wakey."

"What day is it?" I mumbled irritably.

"Saturday."

"Next Saturday?"

"No, this Saturday, silly. No one can actually sleep for a whole week."

My leaden limbs and fuzzy head emphatically disagreed. I rolled to the other side of the bed and slapped another pillow over my head. The earthquake increased in intensity.

"Oh, for the love of marshmallow peeps! Somebody better be dying." I tossed the pillows to the floor and sat up, knuckling the sleep from my eyes. Gran cleared her throat, and I noticed the old woman in a floral housedress, her hair tightly wound in pink, plastic rollers, perched on the foot of the bed wringing her hands together. "Oops. Sorry, Mrs. Colton. No disrespect intended."

"So, the stories are true? You really can see dead people?"

"Are you dead?"

"According to the coroner who is currently zipping me into a body bag? Yes. Dead as disco."

"Well, then, I guess the stories are true."

Praise for Sharon Saracino

The Max Logan Series—2015 Paranormal Romance
Guild Reviewers' Choice Nominee
for Best Paranormal Series

~*~

SMITTEN WITH DEATH—2016 Maple Leaf Award
Winner

~*~

ANGEL IN WAITING—2016 RONE Nominee

~*~

"Characters that jump off the pages with charisma, plot that drives forward at just the perfect pace, and a story that sucks the reader right inside"

~InD'Tale Magazine

~*~

"With tremendous humor and a sharp wit, Sharon Saracino offers a look at what soul searching is all about…"

~Readers' Favorite Book Reviews

~*~

"Witty, insightful, and frequently hilarious, Saracino's writing keeps me up late into the night, chuckling and cheering into my blankets. This series has quickly become one of my favorite reads!"

~AJ Nuest, author of She's Got Dibs

Dedications

For Beverly Melnick, nurse extraordinaire,
incomparable educator, and sorely missed friend.
I hope Heaven has Jell-O in every color of the rainbow.
Except yellow. (By the way, you were right.)

~*~

My gratitude to Susan Letukas
for your effortless wit and memorable one-liners.
May the girls stay perky and may you never suffer
the heartbreak of Cooper's Droop.

~*~

Thank you, Kevin Corcoran,
for your unique mortuary wisdom.

~*~

Sharon Buchbinder, Abigail Owen, J.C. McKenzie,
and Maureen Bonatch, you gals rock my world!
Thank you for your insight, expertise, and support.

~*~

For everyone who's never seen, but still believes,
this one's for you!

Chapter One

"Does this shroud make my ass look big?"

There were moments in life that leave an indelible imprint on your brain. Or a permanent scar, as the case may be. You know the ones I mean. Your first real kiss. Sweet Sixteen. Prom. The day the ghost of the reluctantly departed girl who tormented you in high school decided you're her new best friend. Oh, the ghost part didn't bother me. The dead had been attracted to me like cat hair to black wool as long as I could remember. You know what they say about not being able to pick your relatives. I'm sad to report it also applies to spirits.

Six months ago, I blew out my birthday candles, received a Dandy Discounts Shoe Emporium gift card from my parents—redeemable at locations nationwide—and caught a flight back home to Douglasville to live with my gran. Everyone in town thinks she's a few puppies shy of a litter. I'm relatively sure quite a few think the same thing about me. Imagine my delight when I arrived from the airport, stepped across the threshold expecting to be greeted by an old lady in leather pants, and received the unwelcome homecoming gift of Darla Swithers' ghost, instead. The annoying apparition has stuck to me like polyester on a leisure suit ever since and, flat out, refuses to leave. As birthdays go, I've had better.

"Well?" Darla demanded.

I glanced up at the Queen of Mean who'd managed to swivel her head nearly one-hundred and eighty degrees in an attempt to examine the width of her posterior in the full length mirror on the back of my bedroom door. I placed my copy of The Beginner's Guide to Banishing Pesky Poltergeists face down on my bed so I wouldn't lose my place. Yes, I knew she wasn't a poltergeist, but nothing else had gotten rid of her, and my desperation increased daily. Assuming a pseudo-solicitous expression, I gave her tush a critical once-over.

"It's not a shroud, it's a jogging suit. And yes."

I tried to be nice, truly. It's just that since Darla's untimely death, and even more untimely afterlife, my mouth refused to cooperate. I know the Golden Rule says to do unto others as you would have them do unto you. However, since this particular other devoted the better part of high school making my life miserable, I figured it bought me a pass.

"Aren't you ever going to let it go, Lucy?" Darla whined, planting her hands on her hips. "How many times must I tell you, I was young and—"

"Self-centered and thoughtless and stupid," I interjected. "Let's not forget totally, completely, and irrevocably stupid."

"Fine." She rolled her blue eyes and huffed out a breath. "And stupid. Frankly, most people thought you were a little weird anyway. It didn't really seem like such a big deal at the time, you know?"

"I'm not weird. I'm exceptional." Although as a teenager, those two descriptors felt like pretty much the same thing. Mostly, they still did. "Honestly, Darla, if you're trying to justify your bullying, you're doing a piss poor job."

"It wasn't bullying. I was defending my territory. Please note the difference."

"Your territory? As if someone like me posed a threat to anything you had." I slid from my bed and crossed my arms over my chest as she turned back to the mirror and continued trying to apply mascara as though I hadn't spoken.

Darla's brows drew together. I thought they could use a waxing, but she claims it's impossible to maintain regular upkeep in the afterlife. Unlike the cool, defensive expression she usually wore—which worked beautifully with the upscale zombie look she was rocking—at the moment, she simply appeared exhausted. My heart ached a little. Sure, I was bitter. But lately, I found my antipathy mitigated by pity. Yes, she'd made my life miserable. However, in the end, I had the rest of mine in front of me. She didn't. Darla's hopes, dreams, and possibilities ended forever with an anaphylactic reaction to Botox at the tender age of twenty-six. Even dead, she retained the ability to push most of my buttons. But let's face it. Death by Cosmetic Botulism Toxin is too sad for words.

"You should get dressed. It's getting late. We have to go." Her eyes met mine in the mirror and darted quickly back to her own reflection as she swiped a finger beneath her lower lashes capturing an imaginary smear. I figured it must be an unconscious habit because Darla couldn't actually *apply* my makeup being, you know, dead. But, though her thick, blonde curls still looked great, dissatisfied with her final, eternal makeover, she spent fruitless hours at my vanity table trying to make improvements.

"I'm already dressed. And I told you, you aren't coming."

"You aren't planning to wear *that*, are you?" She turned from her intense contemplation of her own appearance, and zeroed in on mine. One brow quirked into an artful half-moon as she surveyed my blue surgical scrubs with Good Samaritan Emergency Department emblazoned in white embroidery over my left breast, and my well-worn leather tennis shoes.

I glanced down. "What's wrong with it?"

"Seriously? Look at me." My antagonist pointed to her ensemble. "Do you think if I had any inkling I would die and have to wear this fuzzy purple monstrosity for all eternity I wouldn't have chosen more carefully? You could walk out the door and get hit by a bus, and *that'd* be what you'd be stuck with. Where's the outfit I picked out for you? If you want to attract a man, you have to dress the part. Something short and sexy."

"I'm a nurse, not a stripper. Besides, I'm already short and sexy," I snapped back. Because I, you know, totally was. Short, anyway. Okay, maybe not short, exactly, but definitely not statuesque, either. Sexy? Well, I guess some people might consider my eyes an attractive shade of green, and my lashes were long and thick. I kept my dark hair barely long enough to scrape back into a ponytail, because I was all about low maintenance these days. Though it might not be the long, luxurious mane a man itched to run his fingers through, I liked to think the shorter style suited my small face and delicate features. Curves? Not so much. I guess if there's a man out there whose cylinders fire at the sight of an average, no frills woman with minimal cleavage, I might just be his cup of sexy. "Besides, I'm working, not speed dating."

"You look hot in anything, Lucy. Pay no attention to Her Royal Bitchiness, over there. You just wear whatever makes you feel comfortable."

"Um, thanks, Grandpoppy." While I appreciated the support, need I elaborate on the creep factor involved when one's deceased grandfather materializes in the corner of one's boudoir offering impromptu observations on one's sex appeal? I mean, let's face it, that's just not comfortable on any level. "What's new in your little corner of the afterlife?"

"Off to see the pyramids. Last item on my bucket list." He fixed his gaze on me and sighed. "Then I guess it's time to move on."

"Gran will be sorry to hear it." A man who'd dreamed of seeing the world and never managed to travel any further than the annual family vacations at the Jersey Shore, Grandpoppy had been dodging the light for over six years. I knew his soul was long overdue to exit this mortal plane, but I'd grown accustomed to his frequent visits and entertaining travelogues. "I'll sure miss you, though. You'll pop back in to say good-bye to Gran and me before you cross over, right?"

"Count on it, kiddo." He raised two fingers to his forehead in a ghostly salute and began to fade out.

"And don't forget animals can see you," I called out after his rapidly dissolving form. "No teasing the camels. I hear they're mean suckers when they're riled."

"Her Royal Bitchiness? I don't think your

grandpoppy likes me much." Darla pouted.

"Darla." I sighed. "Of course, my grandpoppy doesn't like you. Why would he? You made my high school years a living hell. And not to be rude, but you must realize you aren't *my* favorite person, either. In fact, I honestly don't understand why you insist on hanging around. You wouldn't be caught dead in my company when you were alive. Surely, there must be someone waiting on the other side who'll be happier to see you than I am."

"Tons of someones." She sniffed. "In fact, I wouldn't be surprised if they make me an angel as soon as I get there. I mean, I *am* Darla Swithers, after all. I'm the richest, prettiest, most popular girl in Douglasville."

"And modest. Don't forget the most modest girl in Douglasville." I smirked, scraping my hair atop my head and securing it with an elastic band. Ignoring the goose bumps rising on my arm as I reached through Darla, who appeared annoyingly unaffected, I snatched my keys from the dresser. I shoved them in my pocket and headed for the door. Gripping the doorknob, I stopped without turning around. "Here's the bottom line, Darla. No matter how rich or pretty or popular you were in life, no matter how long you linger and try to avoid it, you're dead now. I'm sorry about what happened to you, but I can't change it. No one can. You need to find a way to accept it and move on. I promise you'll be much happier once you do."

"What if you're wrong?"

Unable to ignore the tremulous note in her characteristic nasally whine, I released the knob with a sigh and turned to face her. I *so* didn't have time for this right now.

"What?"

"What if you're wrong? What if I'm not happier? What if I go into the light and discover I'm damned instead? Death gives a person a whole new perspective, you know. I understand now I may not have been...particularly nice. But you have to admit, the idea you could actually see and talk to the dead really did make you look like you were crazy. I had to work with what I was given. Since we are having this conversation, clearly you aren't. Crazy, I mean. I am a big enough person to admit I was wrong. So, I'm sorry."

I simply stared. An immediate response escaped me. If I had a tiara handy, I might have crowned her the Queen of Understatement. *Not particulary nice*? Spoiled, catty, and cruel, with a hefty dose of entitled thrown in for good measure, perhaps. Still, she did look genuinely repentant at the moment. Hands clenched in front of her, eyes downcast, her spirit flickered nervously like a candle in a breeze. Maybe she actually *was* sorry for all the grief she'd caused. And maybe she was simply scared of the price she might have to pay beyond the light and wanted to hedge her bets. That sounded more like the Darla I knew and despised.

In any event, I wasn't an insecure teenager anymore. I refused to apologize, lie, or be embarrassed. I didn't intend to rent a billboard and announce my, um, special gift. However, if the subject came up, I didn't plan to hide it anymore, either. If people believed me, fine. If they didn't, I could understand that, too. If they thought I was crazy? Maybe it said more about them than about me. I'd reached a comfort level with myself and my ability—mostly—and I didn't need anyone's approval. Darla clearly did. Funny, what goes around apparently does come around. Well, if it took my forgiveness to give her some sort of peace—and more importantly get her out of my life once and for all—I would happily slap on the adult hat in this increasingly dysfunctional relationship and bestow it.

"No, you weren't especially nice." I cleared my throat to avoid choking on my words. "However, it was a long time ago, and you're right. You were young. And while I realize it must have been a bit unnerving to discover me carrying on a conversation with someone you couldn't see, you could have kept it to yourself. Still, we're both adults now. The past is in the past. So, I forgive you." Okay, maybe I wasn't entirely sincere, but I figured death didn't suddenly make Darla psychic.

"Truly?" Her eyes widened and a slow, ghastly grin spread across her face. I felt the tiniest twinge of guilt and genuinely hoped she wasn't planning to rely on her looks in the afterlife.

"More or less. We can't change the past, Darla, we can only learn from it. I have. I hope you have, too. So, go ahead, go into the light, and rest in peace. It'll all be fine."

"That is *such* a relief." Darla floated up to the ceiling as though a weight really had been lifted, before zooming back down to hover in front of me. "Now I can go into the light without fear. And I will, just as soon as I fix things."

"F-f-fix things?" I stuttered in a horrified tone. My heart kicked me in the ribs. Did she intend to stick around? She was supposed to leave, vamoose, get lost. I wondered if I could afford a reputable exorcist. "What are you talking about?"

"Just because I can't change the past, doesn't mean I can't influence the present, right? I may be the one who's dead, but let's face it, your social life is barely limping along on life support. Though I didn't do much to help the less fortunate in life, it's not too late. I can still make it up to you."

Ordinarily, I love storms. The raw forces of nature colliding with a bone rattling crash quickly followed by a flash of hair sizzling brilliance appealed to me on a purely visceral level. But this was no wondrous meteorological event. This was Hurricane Darla, intent on *helping* me. I doubted I had an umbrella big enough for this downpour. Wait a minute. Had she just implied *I* was the less fortunate?

"I know it must be difficult to accept, but facts are facts. You're dead, Darla. It wasn't the butler. The Botox did it. And if I'm lacking a social life, it may be due in large part to your gossip, leading people to believe my elevator doesn't go to the top floor. Anyway, I came back to town to help my gran, not become a social butterfly. I've accepted the fact my ability probably rules out romance. I'm perfectly happy exactly as I am." My voice rose with every syllable until it reverberated loudly enough to rattle my own eardrums. Panic has that effect on me. "I don't need you to…"

"This will be so much fun." Her voice lingered in the air as she faded from sight. "Trust me. You won't be sorry."

Heaven help me, I already was.

Chapter Two

Nothing more interesting than the typical bumps, bruises, and a stomach bug or three swooshed through the automatic doors of the Good Samaritan Emergency Department for the first seven and a half hours of my eight-hour shift. With less than thirty minutes remaining before I could pursue an intimate encounter with my pillow-top mattress, all hell broke loose. Naturally.

The trauma alert crackled over the radio—a multivehicle accident involving several cars, a tractor trailer, and a school bus carrying a high school baseball team—minutes before the first confused spirit streamed through the doors, along with the gurneys and paramedics. My stomach plummeted into my sneakers. I averted my gaze from the bewildered specter of the wide-eyed teenager curiously observing the chaos from the corner of the waiting room ceiling. Blinking away the tears pricking the back of my lids, I swallowed over the lump in my throat and forced my brain into triage mode. I couldn't do anything to save that kid, and there were others in need of my help.

Four hours, three deaths, and eight surgical consults later, I provided a handoff report on my patients to the relief staff and called it a night. Although calling it a morning would have been more accurate.

I hadn't seen Darla since arriving for my shift, but

as I schlepped in the direction of the locker room, I noticed her hovering outside a trauma bay at the end of the hall. A quick glance through the gap in the curtain as I passed explained her confounded expression. Reclining against the elevated head of the gurney, I glimpsed Harlan Hampton IV, Darla's recently widowed husband. His features were set in tense lines as the doctor applied a dressing to his right arm.

I hadn't seen Harlan and his companion come in, so didn't know if his car had been involved in the wreck, or his presence was due to a completely unrelated predicament. Given her stricken expression, I assumed Darla perceived his injuries as more serious than they appeared. Or she didn't recognize that, as I did, the voluptuous redhead clinging to Harlan's plaster-free hand and spilling over the top of her painted-on dress, was his clear and obvious attempt to camouflage his grief over his recent bereavement.

At least that's the theory I planned to extrapolate if anyone, such as Harlan's reluctantly departed spouse, asked my opinion. My already low estimation of Harlan Hampton IV took a nosedive. I doubted she would ever be my favorite person, but even Darla Swithers deserved better than a hooker in hoo-ha heels assuming her rightful place before the grass had time to sprout on her grave.

With no desire to risk being sucked into conversation with Harlan, I stumbled past the cubicle and slipped into the locker room, relieved to find it empty of both the living and the dead. I leaned against the door for a moment enjoying the familiar scent of mildew, disinfectant, and stale sweat. Then I levered myself upright, retrieved a fresh set of scrubs from the rack inside the door, and headed for the showers.

Cranking the water to a temperature slightly below boiling, I stepped under the showerhead and turned my face up to the stinging needles, allowing the soothing spray to wash the grief and tension of the last few hours down the drain. Lather, rinse, repeat. I knew I couldn't save everyone, and my unique perspective into the helplessness of souls traumatically set adrift from their lives in the blink of an eye sometimes made my job doubly difficult. So, I tried to focus on those I could help. Thankfully, tonight there had been more of the latter than the former.

Wisps of steam rose from my heat-pinked skin as I stepped from the stall and briskly scrubbed myself dry with the rough hospital towels. I crawled into clean clothes and rummaged in my locker for my purse. I closed the door with a click, and then rested my aching head against the cool metal with a sigh as a timid voice piped up behind me.

"Am I dead?"

I turned slowly to face the spirit of the teenager flickering uncertainly at the end of the aisle. I set my purse on the wooden bench between the rows of lockers and sank down, perching my tired ass next to it. I'd been hoping some deceased loved one would make an appearance and explain it to the poor kid before I had to. I've discovered when death comes without warning, it sometimes takes the denizens of the afterlife a little time to get their act together.

"I'm sorry. I'm afraid you are."

"Well, that sucks. I'll miss the all-star game. My dad is going to be pissed."

I doubted the all-star game would be his father's

primary concern. I thought it best to keep it to myself.

"So, if I'm dead, how come you can see me?" he asked.

"No clue." I shrugged. "It's something I do."

"Cool." He grinned.

"Sometimes. Sometimes not so much." Like now. At the moment, definitely not so much. This kid might consider himself a big, strapping jock, but he was only a baby. Somebody's baby. Though I couldn't change it, I didn't have to like it.

"So where do I go, now?" His smile faded, replaced by an uneasy frown.

Why did they always assume because I could see them, I had all the answers? This ability didn't come with an instruction manual. I wasn't a spiritual travel agent. I had no idea where anyone went. I only knew the first step to getting there.

"Do you see a light?"

"I think so. Wait, wow…yeah. It's so bright. Uncle Bob? Hey, Uncle Bob! No, I won't pull your finger. I figured that trick out years ago." He squinted into the empty room behind me, and an expression of relief replaced the apprehension. Then he looked back at me with a smile. I released the pent up breath I'd been holding. "Thanks, Lucy."

"I didn't do anything. Hey, how do you know my name?"

"Don't know. Just do. Hey, if you ever run into my folks, can you tell them I'm okay? And I love them?"

If I had a nickel for every spirit who made that request…well, I wouldn't be a millionaire, but I'd have a hell of a lot of nickels.

"Sure, kid. If they ask," I promised, watching him

fade from sight and letting myself off the hook in the process. Because if I actually did run into his folks, why would they ask? The concept of my ability remained so far outside most people's reality even the high school gossip girls didn't actually *believe* I saw dead people. The fact I believed it? That branded me a squirrel. Gran's eccentricities only compounded the situation. Once, I assumed my ability had a higher purpose. Not anymore. Now, I understand people need to navigate their own course through the dark sea of loss. I know this because I've discovered delivering an unsolicited final message from the dearly departed more often results in a restraining order than any real comfort for the bereaved.

Marveling at my continued ability to move after the endless hours on my feet, I swung my leg over the bench and hauled myself upright. Okay, maybe I caught my foot on the bench, lost my balance, and slammed my shoulder into the lockers, however I did ultimately manage to achieve verticality. Slinging my bag over my shoulder, I stepped out into the hall. As usual, a few spirits aimlessly wandered the corridor—it is a hospital, after all, and not everyone makes it out alive.

I've never figured out why some of the deceased seek my company, while others don't. As a rule, most spirits and I acknowledged one another without engagement, like polite strangers on an elevator. I looked up and down the hallway and saw no sign of Darla. After months of trying to rid myself of her tenacious and unasked for presence, why did my stomach now churn with unease at her absence? Dare I hope she finally decided to cross over? Then I remembered her pained expression as she lingered outside Harlan's cubicle. Maybe she actually loved the pompous ass. I guess I'd never considered a person's heart could break once it stopped beating. I briefly contemplated the notion ditzy Darla might be growing on me when I found myself hoping she hadn't decided to leave just yet. I didn't want Harlan and his hoochie mama to be her last memory of this world.

The radio crackled to life through the overhead speakers, reminding me things were about to get busy again, and not in a good way. It was time to make tracks and get out of here. If Darla's spirit still lingered in the ED, she knew the way home. She didn't need me to give her insubstantial butt a ride. Tuning out the trauma alert and concentrating instead on the sound of my bed calling my name, I dug in my bag for my car keys and plowed through the exit door. Where I promptly crashed into a broad chest as forgiving as a concrete construction barrier.

I fought to maintain my balance, my arms flailing like a windmill in a category three hurricane—I can usually achieve a category five, but it had been a long night. Regardless, my rump would have kissed the cold, hard pavement if a pair of strong hands hadn't gripped my shoulders and hauled me against the aforementioned concrete construction barrier to keep me upright. I gasped, enveloped by the pleasing aroma of freshly washed cotton mingled with the salty clean tang of a warm ocean breeze. I admit I found the scent very appealing. Almost as appealing as my body pressed tightly against six feet of rock solid man muscle. Before I had a chance to appreciate the sensation fully, he opened his mouth, and the annoyance dripped from his words like a bucket of ice water dashed over my head.

"You should watch where you're going."

I wrenched free, stepped back, and gazed at the living, breathing embodiment of my every fantasy. Dark eyes, topped by darker brows, which were presently knit together in an impatient frown, stared down at me. High cheekbones, a classically chiseled jaw dusted lightly with five o'clock shadow, and full, sensual lips completed the picture, along with tousled, dark hair that looked as though he'd been combing his fingers through it. Or had just rolled out of bed.

Figures I'd run into—literally—the man of my dreams at the end of an unanticipated fourteen-hour shift, feeling like a wrung out dishrag and looking worse. Still, he didn't have to be an asshat about it. A flush of humiliation heated my cheeks and crept up my face to the roots of my hair. I quickly bent to gather the disseminated contents of my purse, along with my scattered wits, as blood pounded in my ears.

"Maybe *you* should watch where *you're* going."

To my surprise, he laughed. "Yeah, maybe. Sorry. Here, let me give you a hand."

"O-o-o-o, yes, let him give you a hand." Darla's high-pitched squeal startled me enough to drop the items I'd started to scoop into my bag. "And any other body part he'd care to offer."

"Get lost," I hissed under my breath. Had I actually thought she was growing on me? Yeah, like an infected boil on my ass.

"Hey, I said I was sorry. You're the one who came barreling through the door hunched over like Quasimodo."

"I wasn't talking to you," I snapped without

thinking. I straightened and flushed all over again, snatching three tampons and a pack of gum from his unresisting fingers and shoving them in my pocket. I bit my lip to hold back the grin as he regarded me intently with a puzzled expression and made a big show of looking around the parking lot, swiveling his head from side to side and craning his neck in every direction.

"Pretty sure I'm the only one here." His dark gaze returned to mine.

"Looks that way, doesn't it? Sorry, it's been a long night."

"Drop your purse again. Men love a woman in distress," Darla urged. I straightened my spine and ground my molars together, wanting to kill her. However, that would be redundant. I settled for a malevolent glare. To give her credit, Darla could take a hint. She disappeared.

"I heard. It's why I'm here, actually." He stuck out a hand, and after a moment's hesitation, I took it. A jolt of awareness shot from my fingertips up the length of my arm. "Jackson Merritt."

"As in Merritt's Parlor of Eternal Rest?" As if I didn't know.

"One and the same. My crew is pulling around to the morgue entrance as we speak."

"I thought the victims were from out of town?"

"They are. It's illegal to transport a body across state lines unless it's been embalmed. We'll do the initial preparation, and the designated funeral directors will take it from there."

"Ah, I see. So, Jackson Merritt. I thought you looked familiar." As well he should. Knowing he moved in Darla's inner circle and was out of my league didn't stop him from figuring prominently in any number of my teenage fantasies. Hey, a girl can dream. "I graduated with your younger sister. I'm Lucy Ashcroft."

"Lucy Ashcroft..." A spark of recognition lit his gaze. "The Ghost Gabber. I remember you."

"Undoubtedly." I hoisted the strap of my bag higher on my shoulder and lifted my chin. So much for tall, dark, and dreamy. Just when I thought I'd risen above it, there went my reputation preceding me again. Darla wanted me to get a man? It wouldn't happen in *this* town. "Well, as I said, it's been a long night, and I'm sure you have things to do, so..." I tugged at my hand. He didn't release it.

"Yeah, duty calls. Nice bumping into you, Lucy Ashcroft. I hope we can do it again, sometime." Before I could untie my tongue to offer a witty retort, he released my hand with a smile that turned my bones to butter. Then he stepped around me and strode into the hospital.

Chapter Three

I navigated the gloomy, winding road leading from the hospital toward the intersection with the main route back into Douglasville, surrounded on either side by dark, ominous woodlands. The cool, evening breeze whipping through the open windows made me shiver, and the blasting radio rattled my teeth, but the discomfort kept me wide awake, exactly as planned. I heaved a sigh of relief as the lights of Main Street finally came into view. Almost home. Then I made the mistake of glancing in the rear-view mirror just as Darla popped into the back seat, jangling nerves stretched taut by fatigue, and scaring the bejesus out of me.

My foot hit the brake, painting the pavement with twenty feet of burnt rubber skid marks. I wrestled the car to a shuddering halt on the shoulder of the road. The dull ache behind my eyes exploded into a jackhammer concerto as my head became close personal friends with the steering wheel. Peanut Butter Fudge! That was going to leave a mark. Slapping my frozen fingers to my forehead as a makeshift ice pack, I closed my crossed eyes and swallowed hard, willing the stale donuts I'd scarfed down around one in the morning to remain in my stomach.

"What the bloody hell?" Darla exclaimed.

I slowly turned my head and cracked open a lid to

find Darla reclining in the passenger seat.

"You aren't the queen, Darla. You've never been to Britain. If you must swear, please do it like the proud Pennsylvania girl you once were. I think you just made me take an inch of rubber off of my new tires."

"Sorry. So, did Jackson Merritt ask you out?"

"No, he didn't ask me out. And I doubt I would have accepted if he did."

"Are you insane?"

"No, I'm not insane. But I bet he thinks I am." I sighed, edging the car back onto the road. "He was a member of your inner circle, after all."

The old rumors made me hesitant to return to Douglasville. But with Gran getting up in age, my parents and I agreed she shouldn't be alone. When I was a kid, I had no idea my friends were ghosts. I thought everyone saw the things I did. For years, my parents blamed it on a child's imagination. Gran never doubted me. She was always there when I needed someone. And now *she* needed someone. So, I stiffened my spine, put on my big girl panties, and hopped on a plane. Sticks and stones and all that, right? What a surprise to discover names *could* still hurt me. They flew into my ear and stung like hornets. Not as painful as they once were, perhaps, but definitely uncomfortable.

"Clearly, he's familiar with crazy Lucy the Ghost Gabber, the lovely nickname you bestowed upon me," I continued. "Haven't heard it in years. Haven't missed it, either. I don't particularly care to be asked out to appease someone's morbid curiosity. No matter how gorgeous he is."

"Oh, he heard the stories. Straight from the horse's

mouth, I must confess. I think he thought they said more about me, than you. Our parents were friends, and we sort of grew up together though he was a couple of years older. He told me to stop trying to build my own happiness on someone else's misery. He always saw right through me. Of course, I guess everyone sees through me now. In fact, no one sees me at all. No one except you, I mean. Ironic, don't you think?" Darla turned her face away and looked out the window. Then she exhaled softly and disappeared.

The remainder of my trip home remained uneventful. Thankfully. I pulled into the driveway and clicked off the ignition with a sigh. I had neither the energy nor the brain cells to deal with Darla and her belated self-awareness and regrets tonight. Maybe later, after hours of sleep, and massive quantities of caffeine. She had a point, though. The one person she'd been so intent on destroying turned out to be the only person she had left in the end. Ironic indeed.

I climbed out of the car, my head pounding like a competitive Whack-a-Mole tournament had commenced inside my skull. I dragged my butt up the crooked, wooden steps, wanting nothing more than to gulp down a fistful of aspirin and renew my acquaintance with my pillow. The smell of smoke scorched my nose-hairs seconds before the storm door cracked me in the head. As my ass hit the porch, sending a jolt of pain from my tailbone to the base of my possibly fractured skull, Gran barreled out of the house, chanting like a rapper, and brandishing a fistful of smoldering sage in front of her like a weapon.

"Are you crazy? Don't just sit there looking pretty. Get in the house and stay there while I deal with this loathsome creature!" Gran bellowed at me, stomping across the porch in the direction of the porch swing, and waved the smoking bundle in front of her. "Get thee away, you evil bag of bones!"

"One of us is crazy, that's for sure," I muttered as I clawed my way up the porch post until I achieved a semi-upright position. I prodded the left side of my forehead to assess the size of the lump, decided I would live, then ignoring Gran's directive to go into the house, I squinted through the smoke and darkness. On the outermost perimeter of the dim circle of light cast by the bare bulb dangling over the front door, Grandpoppy sprawled on the peeling wooden swing. While I could see ghosts, Gran could only sense them. Problem was, she couldn't distinguish one from the other; so in the interest of self-preservation, she assumed they were all up to no good.

The swing swayed back and forth as she approached, and Gran halted. Grandpoppy cackled in delight. She aggressively thrust the burning bush in his direction. "Be gone, you pencil-dicked spawn of congealed pond scum."

Concerned she might actually injure herself—or set the house on fire—I sighed and shuffled across the porch to wrestle the burning bouquet from her wrinkled, beefy fist.

"Beulah, my bodacious buttercup! You're looking particularly fetching this evening." The only thing more astounding to me than Grandpoppy's comparison of my gran to a buttercup, bodacious or otherwise, was the notion anyone on the planet found leopard print leggings, a purple tank top, and red cowboy boots on a bra-less, overweight octogenarian fetching. I'd like to tell Grandpoppy he looked particularly fetching, too, but as usual, with his stringy gray hair, hollow cheeks, and bejeweled fingers, he had the appearance of an aging rock star who'd been ridden hard and put away wet. They made quite a pair. I guess that's love. Or something.

"Hey, Gran? It's Grandpoppy. He says you look nice." Gran unclenched her fist, allowing the still smoking sage to drop to the porch, and I stomped it out. Then she planted her hands on her hips.

"Oh, that's all right, then." She offered me a gummy grin.

"You lost your dentures again?"

"Lost is such a strong word, Lucy. It implies I have no idea where they are. I know exactly where they are, of course. It's simply a matter of remembering precisely where that is. So, where's Grandpoppy off to this time?"

"Well, er…" I glanced at my grandfather. "He's just come back from Egypt."

"You didn't tell her?" He shook his head and sighed.

"Some of us have to work for a living. The opportunity didn't exactly present itself." I crossed my arms over my chest. It wasn't fair. Why did I have to be the bearer of bad news?

"I hope he wasn't teasing the camels. I hear they're mean suckers. A guy could lose a finger. You still have all your fingers, Eugene?" Gran shouted loudly enough to be heard downtown. In a bar. With the band playing. No matter how many times I reinforced it, she never quite grasped the concept the dead weren't hard of hearing. She didn't need to broadcast into the next dimension to be heard.

"All appendages accounted for," I informed Gran as Grandpoppy held up his hands with a grin and wiggled all ten fingers, his rings twinkling in the dull gleam of the porchlight.

"Well, that's a relief. He's always been good with his hands, you know." Gran winked at me, then turned around, bent her knees, and aimed a couple of well-placed twerks at the porch swing. Lest I go blind, I allowed my head to fall back on my shoulders and stared at the peeling paint on the ceiling instead of the undulating bulges encased in the leopard leggings.

"Gran, some things I really don't need to know, okay?" I counted to ten and risked a glance, relieved to see her keister no longer jiggled. "So listen, it's been six years, right? Grandpoppy's been thinking maybe it's time."

"Time for what?"

"Time for him to, you know, go into the light." The lost expression in her eyes as she gazed up at me broke my heart. I placed a hand on her shoulder and gave it a squeeze.

"Well, that's unexpected."

"I know," I said gently. "And I'll miss him, too. But you know, it must get pretty lonely for him with no one to talk to except me and the occasional cranky camel, right?"

"I suppose. I guess I just thought he'd wait for me, and we'd cross over together." She sighed. "I understand. It's probably for the best."

"She's taking this much better than I anticipated." Grandpoppy frowned, and I nodded.

"And of course, Harold will be thrilled with the

news," she continued, as a mischievous grin plumped her wrinkled cheeks.

"Harold?" Grandpoppy repeated in a puzzled tone.

"Harold?" I prompted, confused myself.

"Oh, didn't I mention Harold?" Gran looked up at me with eyes as wide and innocent as a lamb's. "Harold Granger, down at the Senior Center. He's been hounding me for a little slap and tickle for years. I always felt like it would be disrespectful, knowing Eugene could pop in at any moment. Now he's moving on, well, I may be old, but I'm not dead. A girl's got needs. You understand, don't you, Eugene?"

She batted her lashes in the direction of the porch swing, and Grandpoppy shot to his feet. He zipped across the porch until he stood—or rather, floated— nose to nose with Gran.

"Harold Granger is a bloated, incontinent, asshat with bad teeth," Grandpoppy roared. "If you think for a New York minute I'm going into the light leaving hairy Harold free to paw your magnificent lady lumps whenever he feels the urge, you have another think coming, Beulah Ashcroft. If anyone's looking for me, I'll be in Uzbekistan."

I translated, leaving out the reference to my gran's pendulous bosom. Then the porchlight exploded, plunging us all into darkness, and he disappeared with an outraged crack that made even Gran jump.

"So, I guess he's gone." Gran wrapped her arms around herself and her face crumpled.

"Yep." I draped an arm around her shoulders and steered her in the direction of the door. "To Uzbekistan." Gran skidded to a halt and looked up at me, eyes wide, face wreathed in smiles.

"You mean it worked? I knew it! He never liked Harold."

"Are you saying you made up that whole story to get Grandpoppy to stay?"

"Not entirely. While it's true Harold Granger would give his left nut to get me in the sack, and he's a nice enough guy, he is kind of a bloated, incontinent, asshat with bad teeth. Furthermore, he often reeks of baby powder, stale pee, and dead roses. I may have needs, but I also have standards. Your grandpoppy is a tough act to follow. Think I'll just stick with my BOB."

"Bob?"

"Battery operated boyfriend." Gran winked, lifted her chin, and sashayed into the house, red boots thumping, bra-less boobs bouncing, and leopard butt quivering like chipmunks fighting to get out of a trash bag. I threw up a little in my mouth and dragged my tired ass behind her, reflecting yet again, there were some things—okay, maybe a whole lot of things—I simply didn't need to know.

"Coffee?" Gran called over her shoulder, clomping ahead into the kitchen.

"Going to bed," I called back. I dropped my purse on the table in the entryway, then fished the tampons and chewing gum from my pocket, and tossed them on top. I vowed, as I did at least three times a week, I would clean the unnecessary junk out of my bag today. The damn thing had to weigh upward of twenty pounds, and I was pretty sure a family of four made their home at the bottom. "Do not wake me up, under any circumstances."

"What if it's a matter of life and death?" She appeared in the kitchen doorway and watched me drag myself up the stairs.

"If it's yours, wake me up. If it's mine, let me sleep." I made it to the first landing and regarded the remaining stairs with the enthusiasm of a serial killer facing the electric chair.

"Suppose the house catches fire?"

"Stick to peanut butter and jelly sandwiches until I get up, and it shouldn't be a problem." I made it to the top and leaned against the wall to prepare for the hike to the end of the hall.

"Well, how about—" Her voice floated up the stairs.

"Gran!" I snapped. "Second Tuesday of next week. Got it?"

"Sweet dreams, Lucy." She laughed.

I kicked off my shoes and collapsed on the bed, fully dressed, with all the grace of a falling tree. I briefly wondered where Darla had gotten to and hoped she was all right. But the dark eyes, high cheekbones, classically chiseled jaw with five o'clock shadow, and full, sensual lips hovering on the inside of my lids as I dozed off didn't belong to Darla Swithers. They belonged to someone else, entirely.

Chapter Four

"Lucy, wake up." The mattress shook with the ferocity of a magnitude six earthquake. I pressed the pillow more tightly around my head hoping to muffle the intrusive voice. "C'mon, wakey, wakey."

"What day is it?" I mumbled irritably.

"Saturday."

"Next Saturday?"

"No, this Saturday, silly. No one can actually sleep for a whole week." My leaden limbs and fuzzy head emphatically disagreed. I rolled to the other side of the bed and slapped another pillow over my head. The earthquake increased in intensity.

"Oh, for the love of marshmallow peeps! Somebody better be dying." I tossed the pillows to the floor and sat up, knuckling the sleep from my eyes. Gran cleared her throat, and I noticed the old woman in a floral housedress, her hair tightly wound in pink, plastic rollers, perched on the foot of the bed wringing her hands together. "Oops. Sorry, Mrs. Colton. No disrespect intended."

"So, the stories are true? You really can see dead people?"

"Are you dead?"

"According to the coroner who is currently zipping me into a body bag? Yes. Dead as disco."

"Well, then, I guess the stories are true." I pushed

my hair out of my face and threw back the covers. Glancing at the alarm clock on my nightstand, I was disappointed to discover I'd had less than ten hours sleep. I'd totally been counting on at least twelve. Or eighty-seven.

"Tillie Colton, I can't believe you rushed right over here to tell Lucy you were dead before I got the chance. You always were such a one-upper." Then Gran lowered her voice. "She *is* here, right?"

"Yes, she's here. You can't sense her?" I stuffed my feet into the bedraggled bunny slippers peeking out from under my bed and shuffled toward the bathroom. Gran and the ghost from across the street stayed right on my heels.

"Well, I sensed *someone*. I thought it might be that nasty Darla Swithers."

"I haven't seen Darla since last night. And don't be mean. She's not so bad." I stopped at the bathroom door and turned to face them. "I do not require assistance. Or an audience. Wait right here." I glared at Tillie Colton who I knew was fully capable of passing right through the door, locked or otherwise. "Both of you."

I yanked the drawstring at the waist of my scrub pants and sank down on the padded vinyl seat to relieve my aching bladder.

"Did you mean it?"

"Peanut Butter Fudge, Darla!" I shrieked at the face peering over the top of the shower curtain. "Stop popping up out of nowhere and scaring the crap out of me."

"Fortunately, this time you're prepared." She gestured to my porcelain throne. "So, did you mean it?"

"Mean what?" I jerked up my britches and quickly

washed my hands. Then I made the mistake of glancing in the mirror and scared the crap out of myself. Rummaging in the cabinet drawer, I dragged a brush through my hair and slicked it back into a ponytail. Then I grabbed a washcloth and scrubbed away the mascara crescents under my eyes, and pinched a hint of color into my pale cheeks. Though the improvement was negligible, at least I now looked a little less dead than Darla. Grabbing my toothbrush, I gave my teeth a quick scour and took a slug of mouthwash straight from the bottle. The minty freshness didn't make me feel any more rested, but at least my breath would no longer kill goats.

"You told your gran I'm not so bad."

"Don't let it go to your head. Where've you been?" Before Darla could answer, Tillie Colton stuck her head through the door.

"Get the lead out, Lucy. It looks like they're getting ready to wrap things up over there, and I need you to get the photograph. Oh, hi Darla."

"Hi, Mrs. Colton. Sorry about your untimely demise."

"Honey, I'm ninety-six years old, and I've been bed-ridden for over a year. I think that makes it more of a past-timely demise. Move it, Lucy."

"What photograph?" I asked, pounding down the stairs and out the front door in her wispy wake.

"The photograph I want you to give Jackson Merritt, the mortician. I forgot to include it with my final instructions, and by the time I remembered, I'd become too incapacitated to do it myself, or tell anyone else to. I didn't leave him much to work with, but the photograph will help. It's in the top left dresser drawer in the back bedroom." It was only as we crossed the street, and I found myself approaching Tillie's front porch, that Dr. Monroe, the County Coroner, stepped out the door, and I wondered what on earth I would say.

"Hi, Doc. Listen, I need to get a photograph to give to the funeral director. I kind of promised Mrs. Colton I'd take care of it when she…if she passed."

"Is that so?" He scratched his chin and regarded me oddly. "I thought you only got back into town a couple of months ago."

"Yes, that's right. Six months ago." I smiled and made an unobtrusive attempt to step around him. "And of course, one of the first things I did was stop in to visit Mrs. Colton. She and Gran were such great friends." At least they were until Tillie made a pass at Grandpoppy while in a tequila induced frenzy in nineteen eighty-five. Never let it be said my gran couldn't hold a grudge.

"And that's when she asked you to take care of this?" I had no idea why Tillie Colton materialized behind Dr. Monroe frantically shaking her head.

"Yep."

"Well, now that's real interesting, Lucy. Tillie Colton suffered a massive stroke *eight* months ago and hasn't been able to speak since. She was aphasic."

"Well, she might have mentioned that," I muttered under my breath, glaring daggers at the old bat from beneath my lowered brows. "I mean, oh yes, I know. Expressive aphasia. So sad. It must have been terribly frustrating for her."

"You just said she asked you about this photograph *six* months ago."

"Did I? Well, I just came off a fourteen hour shift

at the ED and had no sooner got my head down than Gran woke me up to tell me about poor Mrs. Colton. I can't be held accountable for anything I say right now. You can relate, am I right? I *meant* to say, Mrs. Colton asked *Gran* to take care of it. Of course, Gran's no spring chicken either, so *she* told *me* about it because she wanted to be sure Tillie's wishes were honored in the event she pre-deceased her. I don't know why Tillie didn't just include it with her final instructions. I guess you'd have to ask her. I suppose it's a little late, is it?"

"Lucy, you're rambling."

"Doc, I'm exhausted." Gazing up at him through my lashes, I pinched the bridge of my nose between my thumb and forefinger and blew out a deep breath. Yes, I was rambling. And doing exactly what I'd sworn I wouldn't when I decided to return to Douglasville. I promised myself I would no longer hide. "You've lived here a long time, Doc. Surely, you've heard the stories about me?"

"That you see dead people? You know, I've been a doctor for forty years, and the county coroner for the last ten. I'd wager I see more death than the average Joe, and I've never seen a ghost. So, yeah, I've heard the stories. Just don't believe 'em."

"Well, that's your prerogative. Believe me or not. It's up to you. Bottom line, Tillie Colton asked me to take care of this. It's a photograph, not the key to her safe deposit box. May I please just get the dang thing for the undertaker and go back to bed?"

"Yeah, I guess so," he said finally, stepping aside to allow me to enter. "But not because I believe you're communing with Tillie's ghost. And make it snappy, kid. You aren't the only one who worked overtime because of that wreck. My bed's been calling my name all day."

"Thanks, Doc. Be back in two shakes."

I darted past him and headed for the stairs, holding my breath against the overpowering odor of raw sewage, barely mitigated by the pervasive scent of mothballs, which hit me in the face and threatened to suffocate me as soon as I crossed the threshold. I trailed Tillie as she streaked along the hallway to the back bedroom, and then I tugged out the drawer she indicated with her long, bony finger.

"How long were you dead before they found you?" I pulled the neck of my scrub top over my nose and took deep breaths through my open mouth.

"Just a couple of hours. There was a mix-up with the home health agency, and the dayshift aide was late. Why?"

"What is that stench?" Gagging, I moved aside a pile of starched linen handkerchiefs embroidered with the letter 'C' to reveal the faded sepia photograph mounted on cardboard lying at the bottom.

"What smell, dear?" Because the odor defied description, I decided to let the matter drop. Frankly, I thought Doc Monroe might want to check for any additional bodies.

"Is this the one?" I held it out for her inspection.

"Yes, it is. People considered me quite a beauty in my day, and that's the way I'd like to be remembered." I turned the photo toward me to have a look. She'd certainly been a beauty. Over seventy years ago. Jackson Merritt might be the hottest thing this side of Hell, but the man was a mortician, not a magician.

"And your day was what? Nineteen forty?"

"I believe it was taken in thirty-eight, dear. Would you like a short tour while I'm still here? This house has quite a history, you know."

"Um, thanks, but I promised the doctor I'd be quick." She had to be kidding. It was an enormous old home filled with oddities and antiques that, ordinarily, I'd love to linger in and explore. But if I didn't get some fresh air soon I would certainly hurl.

"So you did. Well, thank you, Lucy. I appreciate your help."

"Don't mention it, Mrs. Colton. Enjoy your afterlife."

"Aren't you sweet? By the way, if you see anything in the house you'd like, you just help yourself. I left everything to my cat, Mr. Picklepaw. I'm sure he wouldn't mind."

"You left everything to the cat?"

"More or less. I left instructions everything should be sold with the money put into an account for Mr. Picklepaw's care and upkeep for the remainder of his life, and the balance donated to the animal shelter when he joins me. I never married, you know. Not that I didn't have offers. *Plenty* of offers. I'd love to stick around and see the expression on the face of my godson when the will is read. That no-good Harlan IV won't get one red cent from me. Frankly, the boy doesn't deserve the contents of the busted sewer pipe currently spewing shit into the basement."

Well, that explained the smell.

"Wait a minute…are you talking about Harlan Hampton IV?" My mouth dropped open, and I quickly snapped it closed when the odor threatened to become a flavor.

"Yes, I'm sorry to say. Gambled away everything he had, then thought he could get his hands on his wife's fortune. I heard he couldn't pay for her funeral. Her parents stepped in and took care of it."

"I had no idea."

"Well, I don't imagine Darla brags about it. Anyway, I'm off. You can't imagine how wonderful it feels to be free. You tell Jackson I'm counting on him."

"What? Oh, sure. Bye, Mrs. Colton."

She waved gaily and faded from sight. I stuck the photo in the breast pocket of my scrub top, and hiked the neck over my nose again. I hurried down the hall, suppressed the urge to slide down the banister to more quickly escape the reek, and finally burst through the door onto the front porch gasping.

"You didn't think to mention the risk of asphyxiation?" I called, once I managed to take in a few gulps of fresh air. Dr. Monroe straightened away from the black, hearse-like coroner's wagon against which he'd been leaning, and a wide grin split his weathered face.

"Hey, you're the one who claims to have the inside scoop. Didn't Tillie give you a heads up?"

"Ghosts can't smell." Irritated by his condescending tone, I clambered down the steps and pulled the photo from my pocket. "Let me ask you something, Doc. Have you ever seen a million dollars?"

"No." He laughed. "I know everyone thinks doctors make the big bucks, but this county isn't quite that flush."

"However, you don't deny someone somewhere has seen a million dollars?"

"No, I'm sure someone has." He nodded. Then his

eyes crinkled with laughter. "But not many people in this town."

"So, we can agree just because you haven't personally seen something doesn't mean it doesn't exist, right?" His smile faded, and his bushy salt and pepper brows knit together in an inverted V.

"Is that a trick question?"

"Nope." I smiled. "Food for thought. Here's Tillie's photo. Will you see Jackson gets it?"

"Yeah, sure." He nodded, still frowning at me over the top of it. Then he looked down. "For the love of Pete! Merritt's a mortician, not a magician."

"I know, right? She was quite a beauty in her day, though, wasn't she? Nineteen thirty-eight, I believe. Thanks, Doc. Have a good day." I started across the street but stopped and turned when he called out after me.

"You don't actually think he can pull this off?"

"No, I don't." I shook my head and bit my lip, assuming the most serious expression I could muster. "But Tillie sure does."

Chapter Five

I found Gran at the kitchen table happily gumming a peanut butter and jelly sandwich on a hot dog roll. Darla perched on top of the fridge patiently picking up one cereal box after another, as the cat batted them over. I filled a mug from the cold leftover coffee remaining in the pot Gran made when I got home and popped open the microwave. Even stale coffee was coffee in my book.

"Um, Gran? Can you come over here for a sec?"

Gran pushed back her chair and moseyed over to the counter. I swung the door wide.

"Anything in there look familiar?"

"Told you they weren't lost. You really should try to have a little more faith in me, Lucy."

Gran snatched her dentures from the paper plate in the center of the microwave and popped them in her mouth. Then she skedaddled over to rescue the remainder of her sandwich from the mangy orange tomcat who'd jumped to the floor and refocused his attention on Gran's lunch, his whiskers twitching with interest. She shooed him away and resumed her meal.

I reclined against the counter and crossed my arms over my chest as I waited for my twelve-ounce cup of nirvana to heat.

"Gran? When did we get a cat?"

"What? Oh, him. We didn't get a cat. That's Mr.

Picklepaw. He's Tillie's. I've never forgiven her for making a move on Eugene, but we've been neighbors for sixty years. I figured babysitting the old slut's cat was the least I could do. He's got three balls, you know."

"That's awfully nice of you, Gran. However, if Tillie leaves her pet here and goes to the Jersey Shore for a week, it's babysitting. If Tillie dies, I think it qualifies as adoption."

"Good point. Maybe you could pick up a litter box and some kitty treats next time you're downtown?" As though he understood, Mr. Picklepaw leapt into Gran's lap, rubbed the side of his head against her bra-less boob, and began to purr. She reached down to scratch him under the chin with a smile. "And maybe a toy mouse?"

"Sure, why not?" I sighed, tipping a dollop of milk into my day old coffee, hoping this wasn't a tragedy waiting to happen. I didn't want to consider the mess I'd come home to if Gran put Mr. Picklepaw in the microwave and forgot *him*.

"Did you find the photo Mrs. Colton wanted?" Darla asked, as she drifted down from the fridge to settle in the chair across the table.

"Yep. And thankfully, she's moved on. If she hung around waiting for Jackson to make her look like a teenager again, she'd be doomed to disappointment."

"Oh, I don't know," Darla drawled. "He did a wonderful job on me."

"You?" I deftly aspirated a mouthful of coffee and became incapacitated by a fit of coughing. At least, it made it temporarily unnecessary and impossible for me to offer any additional comment. Gran glanced over at the empty chair, while Darla pressed her lips together, arched a brow, and folded her hands on the table in front of her until my imminent respiratory arrest abated. I mean, she didn't look *horrible*. She just didn't look beautiful. Whatever else she'd been, Darla Swithers had been a stunning girl in life. In death? Not so much. "Your, ah, hair looks great."

"Why, thank you, dear." Gran beamed. "I wasn't sure about this perm, but I think it suits me."

"Gran, I was talking to Darla."

"Oh, *her*." Gran's lips twisted in a grimace. "The Botox made her swell up like a puffer fish with hives—at least that's what I heard—but she didn't look half bad once she was all laid out. The Merritt boy does have a way with a corpse. And Darla always did have marvelous hair. So, you don't like the perm?"

"The perm looks fine, Gran."

"I know what you're thinking." Darla sighed. "You're thinking how sad it is that trying to maintain my looks not only killed me but left me a less than attractive corpse."

"I wasn't thinking any such thing," I protested in a wheezy voice.

Darla rolled her eyes.

"Okay, maybe the thought crossed my mind, but you know what I think is sadder? That you believed your worth depended on your appearance."

"Oh, not entirely," she said, rising out of the chair and drifting toward the ceiling. "It also depended on my bank account."

"What else could she believe?" Gran mumbled around the last bite of peanut butter and bread. "Her parents raised her to be a piece of arm candy. Daddy's little princess."

"You can't be a princess forever. Unless of course you actually *are* a princess." I frowned.

"I bet even if you are, everyone fawns all over you while you're around, and then no one has a single good thing to say once you're gone." The sad resignation in her voice made my throat ache. Probably because I knew what it felt like to be followed by whispers, to know everyone talked behind my back. I suspected it was a whole new experience for Darla. Who knew being a princess isn't all it's cracked up to be? For someone who'd disliked Darla Swithers for as almost as long as I'd known her, I suddenly found myself wishing I could fix her life. I couldn't, of course, because her life was over. I knocked back a slug of coffee and cleared my throat.

"You know what they say about eavesdroppers. They never hear anything good about themselves. You should probably stick with Gran and me if you feel like company. At least we're as likely to insult you to your face as behind your back."

"That's quite true. You may not like me, Lucy, but at least you're honest about it. For a weirdo, you have more character than all those snooty debutants who called themselves my friends put together."

"Thanks, Darla. That might be the nicest thing you've ever said to me." Backhanded or otherwise, I appreciated a compliment as much as the next girl.

"Don't let it go to your head. Now, finish your coffee and go make yourself presentable. We're going shopping. Because I'm actually much nicer than you give me credit for, I'm willing to make the sacrifice of scouting ahead to narrow down the choices."

"We are not going shopping. I don't need anything."

"You'll be taking your gran to Tillie's viewing, right? Jackson Merritt is a very hands-on type of undertaker. He will definitely be there. Need I say more?"

"I hate shopping." I groaned.

"I already know you hate shopping. I've seen your wardrobe. Hence, my magnanimous offer to do the advance work."

"Are you going shopping for something to wear to Tillie's wake?" Gran asked. "You will take me to it, won't you? I haven't seen my car keys in months. Not that I *lost* them, mind you. I just haven't remembered where I put them yet."

If she'd bothered to check the garage, she'd realize she hadn't seen her car in months, either. Gran's eccentricity was nothing new. It was one of the things I loved about her. Still, different wasn't dangerous. I noticed it had progressed to more than her usual unconventional behavior as soon as I moved in. The day she strapped on a pair of leather chaps, got behind the wheel, and challenged a local motorcycle club to a drag race down Main Street, we made a trip to the lawyer's office for a gentle, but thorough discussion related to power of attorney. Then I convinced her to allow me to sell the car. She didn't need it anymore. She had me to haul her spandex clad butt around.

"Speaking of Tillie's wake, what exactly are *you* planning to wear, Gran?"

"Oh, don't worry about me. I've got my trusty funeral finery." She rose to her feet and tugged the hem of her purple tank top over her exposed belly and the

41

waistband of her leopard leggings. Then she clomped her cowboy boots over to the fridge and opened the freezer, presumably checking for her keys. "Classic, timeless, and suitable for any season."

"Please tell me there will be no leather or tassels involved."

"Don't be ridiculous, Lucy. It's a funeral, not two-for-one night at the Chinese Buffet. I can do conservative when the occasion calls for it."

"Just checking." I couldn't help noticing she hadn't actually *denied* there would be leather or tassels.

"I *could* use some new pantyhose. As I recall, I last donned my funeral garb for Mabel Griffiths. Darling woman, Mabel. Never flashed *her* garters at my Eugene the way *some* people did. Of course, I weighed at least fifteen pounds less at the time. Queen Size firm control with a double cotton gusset and the invisible reinforced toe should do the trick. If you see any with built in seams, even better."

"See? It's settled." Darla whirled about the kitchen, clapping her hands in glee. "Oh, shopping, how I've missed you."

I slung one leg over the other, my bedraggled bunny slipper quivering in protest. Slumped in my chair, I chugged down my cooling coffee. A trip to the local mall with the ghost of Darla Swithers as my self-appointed personal stylist? I doubted there was enough caffeine in the world.

"Get moving, Lucy. I'll go on ahead while you shower and get changed."

"Why do I need to change? I'm going to be trying on clothes, not walking the runway."

"When assessing fit and fashion, the proper

foundation garments are key. Saggy granny panties and a sports bra do not cut the mustard. I suggest a brassiere with actual support, and maybe a thong to minimize those pesky, and universally unattractive, visible panty lines. As for shoes, anything else you've got will be an improvement. I refuse to be caught dead in the company of someone attempting to pass off roadkill as footwear."

I thrust my scrub-panted leg out from beneath the table and inspected one of my bunny slippers through narrowed eyes. The little black pom-pom nose was missing, and only a couple of fraying threads and a knotted, furry nub remained of the left ear. I decided it was cute in a scruffy, matted, please-put-me-out-of-my-misery kind of way. Still, I'd never wear them out of the house. Okay, maybe I wore them out of the house, but not to the mall.

"Fine, I'll change the shoes and wear a bra. I do not own a thong." I held up a hand as she frowned and opened her mouth. "Nor will I allow you to coerce me into buying one. The humiliation of visible panty lines is far more palatable than the misery of a chaffed ass crack."

"You are a challenge, Lucy Ashcroft." Darla crossed her arms over her chest and lifted her chin. "If anyone can rise to the challenge, it's me. One thing I understand is popular. I know about popular. And I'm going to help you if it kills me."

"You're already dead."

"Semantics."

I bit my lip to refrain from reminding her she'd recently declared no one had anything nice to say about her now that she was gone. How popular could she have been? Still, the country club set had certainly emulated her style and followed her lead when she'd been alive. Even if they hadn't liked her much, they clearly recognized and admired her flair. Once, I'd wanted to be a round peg like them. But I'd always been an octagon with edges that kept me from easily fitting into the traditional hole. Of course, just because I no longer intended hiding my edges didn't mean I had to hone them into weapons either, right? Darla and her questionable friends were all about convention and conformity. Neither of those was my forte. I was more like someone's shot of whiskey than anyone's cup of tea. It didn't mean Darla couldn't teach me a thing or two.

"Okay, fine. I'll meet you at the east entrance to the mall in an hour." I pushed back my chair and carried my empty mug to the sink. "But no thongs."

"I can concede that. Oh, Lucy, this will be so much fun." Darla clapped her hands in glee and disappeared.

I sighed. Shopping with Darla Swithers. Fun wasn't the first word that sprang to mind. Then I thought of Jackson Merritt and resisted the urge to squirm. I'd be lying to myself if I denied I found him attractive. I always had. But we moved in different orbits. He'd been raised in a world of Orange Pekoe and Earl Grey. Dare I hope he secretly craved a beverage with a little more kick?

Chapter Six

After circling the parking lot like a confused buzzard for fifteen minutes, I finally eased the nose of my compact car into a recently vacated spot. Clicking off the ignition and releasing the seat belt, I asked myself for the umpteenth time why I agreed to this expedition. On Saturday afternoon. With Darla. Oh, that's right—tea with whiskey and Jackson Merritt. Slinging my purse, which I had yet to clean out, over my shoulder, I trudged the length of two football fields to the mall entrance. True to her word, as soon as I stepped through the heavy glass doors emblazoned with Douglasville Merchant Village, Darla appeared and outlined the battle plan like a self-appointed general.

"There are forty-seven stores in this mall. In deference to your abhorrence of the joys of retail, I have thoughtfully narrowed our choices to one. Symphony." Her eyes widened, and her brows flew into her hairline as a pained moan escaped my lips. The most exclusive and expensive boutique in town— naturally. "Do you want my help or don't you? Given the state of your closet, I'd suggest you consider your answer carefully."

"Fine," I whispered though clenched teeth and stiff lips. I started walking in the direction of Symphony, which, of course, was located at the opposite end of the concourse.

"Wise choice. Now, after selecting one of the four lovely frocks I've designated for your consideration, we will proceed to Edlebaum's, where we will coordinate shoes and lingerie. Against my better judgment, I've eliminated thongs from the equation. Then, we'll move on to hair and make-up. I would love to let Pasquale get his hands on you. However, in my current state, I found it a bit difficult to arrange an appointment. I did contemplate attempting to show myself at his salon. He's a genius with follicles, but he's a little highly strung. I doubt he would be nearly as blasé about seeing me again as you were. And he carries sharp scissors. Someone could get hurt."

"I agreed to a dress, not an overhaul," I ground out, regretting the entire idea more with each passing minute.

"Darling, style is all about the total package. If you want to tempt Jackson to unwrap the present, you've got to hand it to him with pretty paper and a tasteful bow."

"Did you just compare me to a cardboard box? And who says any of this is about Jackson?"

"Pul-eeze, Lucy. I'm dead, not stupid. And here we are…Symphony!"

I stepped across the threshold, sank to my ankles in the plush, padded carpeting, and found myself in an alternate universe. Instead of the typical fluorescent lighting, subdued radiance gleamed from crystal chandeliers. Classical piano music tinkled softly in the background as I followed Darla's transparent figure to a rack at the back of the store. She halted and gestured to a sleeveless number with an asymmetrical neckline in an impossible to miss shade of fuchsia. I withdrew it from the rack and held it out for inspection.

"Too pink." I mouthed, shaking my head at Darla. I slid the dress back into place at the approach of a saleswoman with her nose held so high in the air, she ran the real risk of drowning in the event of a sudden rainstorm.

"Can I help you?" Her tone implied she'd rather eat glass, while her eyes slowly surveyed me from the top of my messy ponytail to the toes of my grimy tennis shoes.

"Actually, my stylist already texted the choices she'd like me to consider. Thanks ever so much."

"*You* have a stylist?" She coughed, eyes widening.

"Doesn't everyone?" I turned my back in a clear sign of dismissal and moved to the next rack where Darla hovered near a chiffon floral number with yards of ruffling around the full hem and low neckline. "I'll let you know if I need you."

"Oh, well done! You certainly put her in her place."

"It was a knee jerk defensive reaction to her automatic judgment of me based solely on my appearance." I sighed, shaking my head at frock number two. "Too frou-frou. It's a viewing, not an afternoon cotillion. Answering her condescension with attitude of my own wasn't the appropriate way to handle it. I should probably apologize."

"You should do no such thing. Trust me. She wouldn't appreciate it, anyway. And it isn't as though you lied. You do have a stylist. Me. And I am excellent at it. What in the hell is wrong with this one?" She threw her hands in the air as I vetoed her third choice.

"It's just not me."

"Excuse me for articulating the obvious, but isn't that the whole point of this little girls' day out?"

I opened my mouth, intending to tell her maybe I wasn't cut out for *haute couture*. I would just wear my black slacks and a blouse, as I'd originally planned before I let Darla talk me into this exercise in futility. Then, on a shapely mannequin at the back of the store near the clearance rack, I saw it. The Dress. Black, classic lines, wide, scoop neck, and three quarter length sleeves. It caught and held my gaze, and I moved toward it like a cow caught in the rays of an alien's tractor beam. It's entirely possible I also heard angels sing. It was difficult to tell over the ear piercing sound of my self-appointed stylist's horrified screech.

"*Nooooo*. Step away from the clearance rack. Step *away* from the clearance rack."

I reached out and reverently stroked the fabric, while Darla swatted ineffectually at my fingers. I knew it probably wouldn't look as good on me as it did on the plaster goddess, but it couldn't hurt to try it on, right? Ignoring Darla's pitiful wails, I shuffled through the rack, found the dress in my size, and tossed it over my arm. Then I marched into the fitting room, slipped into a cubicle, and slammed the door in her face.

I shucked my jeans and sweatshirt and then dropped the dress over my head, loving the way the fabric caressed me all the way down. I adjusted my boobs and tugged the hem into place until it hung just above my knees. Then I took a deep breath.

"Lose the sweat socks." Darla advised from her perch atop the cubicle. Hopping first on one foot, and then the other, I yanked them off and tossed them on the bench with the rest of my things. "Better. Now up on your toes." She twirled a finger in the air. "And turn."

I dutifully stretched up on my toes, ignoring the cramp in my instep, and turned to regard myself in the full-length mirror. My breath caught in my throat. I wasn't vain by nature, but even I could appreciate the way the unrelieved black made my pale skin glow, and my green eyes pop. The wide, rounded neckline emphasized my limited bust and narrowed my waist, giving me the illusion of an actual figure. I barely recognized the woman staring back at me from the mirror. She looked almost…beautiful.

"It's not *horrible*," Darla allowed, circling me slowly and tapping her chin with her forefinger. "With the right accessories…I believe I can work with it."

"I think I love it," I breathed, my eyes meeting hers in the mirror. Then, my eyes were drawn like a magnet back to the stranger reflected in the glass.

"Then you should buy it."

"I should? I should. I will." I snagged the price tag hanging from the sleeve and turned it over. My stomach flipped. "When hell freezes over. This is someone's idea of clearance? For this price, I could buy a sweatshop in a third world country and hire fifty starving orphans to make all the dresses I want. Then I could fly every one of them to Douglasville on a private jet and buy them dinner. The orphans, not the dresses."

"You're overreacting. And perhaps slightly exaggerating. You make decent money, which you work hard for, and you have few expenses. When's the last time you treated yourself?"

"Treating myself is taking a bus trip into the city to see a show. It's not blowing a whole week's pay on one little black dress." But, oh, how I wanted to. I'd never had a piece of clothing make me feel so special in my entire life.

"I know it seems like a lot of money—*to you*—so, maybe it would help if you considered it an investment. Every woman deserves one perfect LBD that makes her feel beautiful. It's black, it's classic, you can dress it up, or dress it down, and it works for any occasion. It's well made, will wear like iron, and will never go out of style. Just think of the money you'll save on the dresses you *won't* have to buy with this one hanging in your closet."

"I guess I hadn't thought of it like that."

"Well, you should. Much as I hate to admit it— mostly because it wasn't my idea—that dress looks stunning on you."

"You only say that because it's true." I ran my hands over the fabric skimming my hips and turned sideways, trying to view myself from every angle. The idea of paying so much for a single article of clothing made my heart flutter into my throat and steal my breath. Still, Darla had a point. This little number could be styled to go anywhere. "So, if I wear it, say, five times—that's five dresses I don't have to buy—it basically pays for itself, right?"

"Sure, let's go with that."

"I mean, what are the chances I'll wear it five times?" I rarely wore dresses, had few occasions to do so. Of course, it didn't mean opportunity might not come knocking on my door.

"I sense you are feeling conflicted."

"Is telepathy some new secret power you've acquired in death?"

"No, I've always had a keen sense of when someone is arguing with themselves out loud." Darla rolled her eyes. "You'd like the decision taken out of your hands so you can blame me for it later."

"Is that what I'm doing?" I bit my lip and contorted my body to examine my backside. No matter how I looked at it, The Dress was three hundred and sixty degrees of awesome.

"Isn't it?"

"Maybe. You always liked to be the leader of the pack, the one calling the shots."

"That was me. Darla Swithers, the richest, prettiest, most popular girl in Douglasville. Setter of trends, instigator of fads, self-centered, insecure bitch clinging to the top of the mountain with ragged, bloody fingernails. Well, you know what they say about being at the top. There's nowhere to go except down."

"*Please*. You were the least insecure person I've ever known."

"Ah, then my evil plan worked." She smiled, but it didn't reach her eyes. "I made a lot of mistakes trying to live up to the expectations of others, or at least their expectations as I perceived them to be. Too soon dead, too late smart. I guess hindsight is always twenty-twenty, right? The dress suits you perfectly. Splurge for once in your life. It's only money, and in the end, it means less than nothing. Trust me, I know. Buy the damn dress and don't you dare regret it. Life's too short."

"I'm sorry," I said, surprised to discover I actually meant it. Darla Swithers, the girl who had everything. At least I always thought she did. Maybe she had less than I, or anyone else, ever suspected.

"Don't be." She waved away my sympathy. "I made my bed. Are you buying the dress, or what?"

I sucked in a deep breath and blew it out.

"I'm buying the dress. But forget about coordinating footwear from Edlebaum's. I have a Dandy Discounts Shoe Emporium gift card, and I know how to use it. We'll be perusing last season's shoes, Darla. Deal with it."

"You're killing me," she whined, reverting to her usual snooty tone and floating back to the top of the cubicle. "I suppose, you being you, cutting back somewhere helps justify the price of the dress. Will you at least reconsider the thong?"

"The thong isn't open for negotiation." I returned the dress to the hanger and began pulling on my clothes.

"You're impossible. Well, then will you at least agree to something more alluring than *those*?" She jabbed a finger in the direction of my perfectly serviceable white cotton undies, making me glad I'd at least chosen a pair with intact elastic. "A woman must build her look from the skin and work her way out. Do you honestly want *that* dress supported by *those* panties?"

"Well, when you put it that way…" Gran always said to wear clean undies when leaving the house, just in case I got in an accident. I suppose if I got in an accident while wearing The Dress, I'd want people to think I had a clue about the appropriate scanties to wear under it. "Okay, Edlebaum's lingerie and Dandy Discount's shoes. Deal?"

"Because I am pleasantly surprised to discover you actually have an amazing, if heretofore untapped and ridiculously well-hidden sense of style, in the interest of learning to become a team player, I will concede the shoes. You're welcome."

I wouldn't swear to it, but I think Darla Swithers and I just had a moment.

Chapter Seven

On our way to the funeral home the next evening, I struggled to keep my eyes on the road. I couldn't stop glancing over at Gran. At least the woman claimed to be Gran. This elegant stranger in the conservative navy blue sheath dress and matching jacket, with pearls, lipstick, and both upper and lower dentures intact, was a woman I hadn't seen in more years than I could count. I mean, she looked like *someone's* grandmother. Just not mine. Of course, I looked rather unlike my usual slave to casual, as well. Frankly, I'm not sure whose jaw hit the floor first when Gran and I met at the top of the stairs, having primped and prepared our respective selves in our separate rooms.

"Are you wearing clean underwear?" Gran asked, while rearranging the contents of her black patent leather clutch.

"Of course. Why?" Not only were they clean, they were black, and lacy, and looked incredibly sexy with the matching push-up bra. Even on me.

"Because if you don't keep your peepers front and center instead of checking out the old bat in the passenger seat, we're going to have an accident. I wouldn't want you to bring shame on the family by flashing less than pristine panties." Considering our reputations in this town, I'm pretty sure the state of our underwear is the last thing people are interested in.

"I promise I won't land us in the hospital." I smiled, turning my attention back to the road. "I just can't get over it, Gran. I don't think I've ever seen you look so nice."

"So normal, you mean?"

"No, I mean nice. Normal is subjective."

"So, you'd have been on board if I wore my zebra striped bell-bottoms and motorcycle boots?"

"Gran, I love you exactly as you are. You should never hide your light under a bushel for anyone. Will it hurt your feelings if I say I'm not sorry you decided to hit the dimmer switch for something as somber as death?"

"Depends." Gran shot me a sly, sidelong glance.

"On?"

"On whether you'll get me a pink feather boa and a shiny tiara for Christmas."

"I guess it can be arranged." I laughed. "They'll go nicely with your rainbow disco wig."

"Exactly what I was thinking." She chuckled. "You know, Lucy, some people in this town think I'm straight up bonkers. Oh, sure I know I'm a little forgetful these days, and I'm more grateful than you know to have you home to make sure I don't do something outright dangerous like burn the house down. But for the most part, I know exactly what I'm doing. Anyone who knows me—truly knows me— knows that. If I've dressed like a clown and sometimes act as if I'm off my rocker over the last ten or so years? Well, it gives the so-called *normal* people in this town something to gossip about. I'm performing a public service, really."

Ahead I saw the Merritt Parlor of Eternal Rest, an

imposing, white Victorian with an enormous front porch trimmed in elaborate wooden scrollwork and surrounded by meticulous landscaping. Large floral arrangements in white, wicker baskets stood guard on either side of the stairs, and a coordinating wreath hung on the front door. I turned into the driveway and followed the waving arm of an elderly gentleman in a black suit to a parking spot in the lot in the back. I shifted into park, clicked off the ignition, and dropped the keys in my purse. Then I turned to the woman beside me, my stomach churning.

"You did it for me." Tears pricked the back of my eyelids. "The outlandish clothes, the crazy stunts, it had nothing to do with age or dementia at all, did it? Ten years ago, when I was in high school, and Darla and the Douglasville Debs were on their smear campaign, you decided if people were talking about you, maybe they wouldn't concentrate on me. That's it, isn't it?"

"I have no idea what you're talking about. I simply think at my age, I should be able to indulge in whatever fashion choices take my fancy. It's fun. If people feel the need to talk, well, I guess they have nothing more productive to do. Isn't that sad?"

"I love you, Gran." I reached over and squeezed her hand, swallowing hard.

"I love you too, Lucy. Now let's get this dog and pony show started. These pantyhose are squeezing my bladder into my tailbone, and as for the bra…well, let's not go there. I do believe my girls are in shock."

"Well, when everyone in there gets a gander at you tonight, your girls won't be the only ones." I laughed. I shoved open my door and then came around to Gran's side to help her out. Pulling her arm through mine, we carefully navigated the flagstone walkway around the side of the house and climbed the front stairs.

"For the record, Lucy, you look stunning. Just remember, different isn't abnormal. And it's a hell of lot more fun than run-of-the-mill. You've just got to be willing to own it." She winked and squeezed my arm as the door swung open from the inside. And there he was. Sex in a suit. Granted, it was a dark, somber suit befitting the occasion, but he wore it like a Milan runway model. Jackson waved us in with a professional smile, and my girly bits quivered in response.

"Ladies."

"Good evening, Jackson," Gran extended a hand. "Beulah Ashcroft. I will, of course, excuse you for not recognizing me. It *has* been a while. How is your dear mother?"

"She's fine, thank you." He took Gran's hand, but his wide eyes were all for me. "Lucy? I didn't recognize you at first with clothes on."

"Excuse me?" Gran tugged her hand from his and glared.

"Street clothes, I meant street clothes." Jackson cleared his throat. "The last time I saw Lucy she was wearing scrubs."

"Oh, that's all right, then." She patted his arm. "Please give your mother my best. Lucy, dear, sign the guestbook for both of us, will you? I'll see you inside."

Gran strutted into the viewing parlor as though she owned the place, leaving me alone in the vestibule with tall, dark, and oh-dear-Lord-what-do-I-do-now? I shifted from one foot to the other, successfully rolling my ankle in the unfamiliar heels. A warm, strong hand on my elbow saved me from an ungainly sprawl. Again.

"Oh, nicely done!' Darla crowed from the banister of the curved wooden staircase leading to the second floor. "Here less than five minutes and you've already got his hands on you. It's entirely possible I underestimated your skills."

I pressed my lips together and jerked my head in the direction of the viewing parlor. Jackson glanced at the stairs and gave me a curious look.

"Crick in my neck. Must have slept on it funny last night. Um, thanks." I looked down at his hand on my elbow and suppressed a shiver of delight. "Haven't worn heels in a while. We like to keep things fairly informal in the ED."

"Well, you should wear them more often. You look beautiful," he countered with a smile. Darla clapped her hands and zipped away in Gran's direction with a giggle. "And your grandmother looks especially, uh, grandmotherly, this evening. I didn't recognize her."

"Well, sometimes conventional is the flavor of the day."

"True, but I sometimes find conventional to be a little on the vanilla side, don't you? I'm more of a butter pecan kind of guy, myself."

"So, you like nuts?" Heat crawled up my neck and flooded my face. Oh. My. God. Did I seriously just ask him about nuts? Does he think I'm referring to *his* nuts? Maybe I should check with the community college and see if they need anyone to teach a class in Flirting 101. Clearly, I should share my skills with the world. "I mean, uh, well some people are allergic, you know."

"Not me." He released my elbow and smiled down at me as he pulled my arm through his. "I think nuts add a unique flavor and texture to what might otherwise be a bland and boring dessert. Let's get you a seat, shall we? The service will be starting soon."

"Okay," replied the Queen of Witty Repartee. I looked up into his dark eyes and promptly forgot how to breathe. I wondered how long a person could tolerate oxygen deprivation before losing consciousness. I'm a nurse. I should know the answer, right? However, at the moment, I could barely remember my own name. Though I'd agreed to descending into retail hell with Darla to possibly capture Jackson's attention—or at least to prove I don't always look like the rumpled paper bag he'd crashed into at the ED—I hadn't honestly believed it would work. And now I seemed to actually *have* his attention, I had no idea what in the hell to do with it.

A cool breeze snaked around my ankles, heralding the opening of the door.

"Jackson, *darling*," the sweet, sing-song voice from my past froze me in my tracks and made the hair on the back of my neck jump to attention. Jackson glanced down at my hand gripping his arm tightly enough to draw blood, even through the fabric of his beautifully tailored jacket, and quirked a dark brow. Lines appeared at the sides of his mouth as he pressed his lips together, before pasting on a smile, and turning the two of us as a unit to face the newcomer.

Bunny Bartley, Darla's former BFF and partner in the denigration of all deemed to be lesser beings, stood poised inside the door. She shifted her mascara-heavy gaze from Jackson, to me, to my hand on his arm, and then back to me again. Recognition widened her blue eyes, and her full, pink lower lip pushed out in a pout. Then she tossed her elegantly coiffed platinum head and clicked her three inch stilettos across the tiled entryway until her generous breasts—pushed high enough to rest her chin on them—were plastered against Jackson's chest.

"Jackson, will you be a dear and help mother? She's waiting around back. You should build a ramp out front, darling. Differently-abled people should not have to feel like the hired help."

"I don't control the zoning ordinances, Bunny. Will you excuse me, Lucy? Why don't you go ahead in and join your grandmother. I'll talk to you later." He put his hand over mine and squeezed before drawing his arm away.

"Uh, sure. Nice to see you, again."

I turned toward the entrance of the viewing parlor, stopping to sign the guestbook for both Gran and me. Which was a mistake. As soon as Jackson disappeared through the back door, Bunny latched on to my upper arm and spun me on my heels.

"Well, well, well. Lucy the Ghost Gabber. I heard you were back in town."

"How exciting for you. I see irrelevant news still travels fast around here. Well, if you'll excuse me—"

"Don't think just because you went away to college and apparently acquired some fashion sense that anyone's forgotten what a freak you are." She lifted her chin and looked down her surgically enhanced nose. I couldn't help noticing the asymmetry of her nostrils as they flared in anger. "And you just stay away from Jackson Merritt, too. I saw the way you were hanging all over him. That man is far too polite for his own good."

"If that's your idea of hanging all over a man, you

have a lot to learn about hanging all over men. Trust me, Bunny, when I hang all over a man, he knows it. And he enjoys it." My lips peeled back in a grin. Funny, this perfect, plastic bitch didn't intimidate me at all, anymore. Maybe I really had become more comfortable in my own skin. Or maybe I was just biding my time until I could wipe the snooty smirk right off of her collagen-injected lips. "Maybe you need to get out more."

"And maybe you need to face facts. If Jackson is being nice to you, it's because it's his business to be nice to people. I realize it's hard for someone like you to understand, but you shouldn't get your hopes up and see it as anything more. He's out of your league, and you have absolutely nothing in common."

"Oh, I don't know. I talk to dead people. He talks to dead people…"

"Well, his dead people don't answer back."

"To be fair, I've never carried on a conversation with a corpse myself, so I'm not actually sure they can. I generally stick to the incorporeal."

"Aha!" She hissed loudly enough to cause several mourners to swivel in their seats and regard her with severe expressions. The annoyance faded from her features, replaced by something that looked suspiciously like triumph. "That does mean ghosts, right?"

"Why, Bunny! Have you been reading the dictionary? Yes, it means ghosts. Ghosts, spirits, apparitions, specters, phantoms…take your pick."

"So, you admit it. You really *do* believe you can talk to the dead. You're just as crazy as ever."

I guess it had been too much to hope any of the

Douglasville Debs would be grown-ups and let sleeping—or talking—ghosts lie. I straightened my spine, and looked her right in her overly made up eyes.

"I may be crazy, but at least I can wear cute sandals. How are the transplanted cadaver toes working out for you, sweetie?" I shook my head and clucked sadly. "Hey, maybe you can get your own reality show. You can call it *When Pedicures Go Bad*."

"H-h-how did you know about that? No one knows. No one except my mother and—"

"And the little ghost who told me."

Chapter Eight

"There! Didn't that feel good?" Darla giggled.

Ignoring her, as well as Bunny's strangled gasp and bloodless cheeks, I spun on my heel and strode into the viewing parlor. She had it coming, right? Unlike Darla, Bunny hadn't learned a thing after all these years. It isn't the lake surrounding the boat that sinks it; it's the water you allow inside. I vowed I would no longer allow people's opinions, least of all Bunny Bartley's, to be the deluge dooming my dingy. I expected to feel vindicated. I didn't. I'd sunk to Bunny's level. And since I knew exactly what it felt like to be on the receiving end, I briefly wondered if it made me even worse than her.

Tillie had lived a good long time, and it seemed as though everyone in town came out to say goodbye. Gran always said the best thing about being from a small town was everyone knew everyone else. Of course, she also said the worst thing about being from a small town was everyone knew everyone else. I agreed in theory with both sides of the argument, the downside of the latter being everyone also knew everyone else's business. And some hung onto it with the ferocity of a starving dog to a meaty bone. I scanned the room and located Gran huddled near the back with a couple of her cronies from the Senior Center, and took my place behind the mourners waiting to view the body and pay their respects.

Despite the crowd, the line moved quickly, and before I knew it, I stood gazing down at Tillie. She looked lovely, her face nearly unlined, peaceful, and rosy against the pillow of ivory satin. I smiled when I saw the gilded frame propped against the lid of the casket along with a nosegay of pink miniature roses. Maybe Jackson hadn't been able to give Tillie the illusion of youth she desired, but he did manage to make her a handsome woman who didn't appear a day over seventy, and I thought it incredibly kind of him to include the photo to ensure everyone knew she'd been a beauty in her day.

"What do you think?" Jackson's deep voice whispered near my ear, his warm breath ruffling both my hair and my composure. Apparently, owning the funeral home came with the added perk of being able to cut the line without inducing a riot. "I don't think I quite managed the look she wanted, but I hope she's pleased."

"No human alive could make a ninety-six year old invalid look eighteen again. You've done a beautiful job. I'm sure she would be pleased." I stepped forward as the line shifted, drawing ever nearer to the principle mourner, Harlan Hampton IV. My palm itched with the urge to slap the serious, sorrowful look right off his face. He didn't give a flying fig about Tillie, and I strongly suspected he hadn't turned out to be Darla's Prince Charming, either.

"Would be? You mean she isn't here? Doc said she gave you specific instructions, and I hoped for a little feedback. The opportunity doesn't often present itself in my line of work." My heart dropped into my strappy new black pumps. I heard the smile in his voice, and my gut twisted. I dared to hope he'd be different. I'd been a fool.

"Excuse me," I whispered and sidestepped out of the line, heading for the back of the room where Gran waited. She looked up as I approached and then glanced behind me. Her eyes narrowed.

"Something wrong?"

"Just tired." I forced my stiff lips into a smile. "Are you about ready to leave?"

"We just got here. Don't you want to stay for the prayer service?"

"I, uh...sure, if you want to." I sighed, looking around for an empty seat.

"You know, Beulah, my daughter is picking me up at nine. I'm sure she'd be happy to drop you at your house if Lucy wants to leave," said Helen Davies, the neighbor from two doors down.

"Oh, how nice of you, Helen." Gran peered up at me. "Maybe I should just go with Lucy."

"It's okay with me if you want to stay, and Mrs. Davies' daughter doesn't mind. I'm fine, Gran. Really." In fact, right about now I'd actually welcome a little solitude.

"Well, if you're sure..." Gran's brows drew together.

"You stay and visit with your friends." I bent and pressed my lips to her tissue paper cheek. "I'll see you at home."

My eyes sought out Jackson's tall, tailored figure as though they had a mind of their own. Thankfully, he was too busy navigating a path for Mrs. Bartley and her walker to notice. I scurried through the foyer and slipped out the door. Digging in my clutch for the car keys, I turned the corner to the walk leading around to the parking lot, and narrowly avoided a collision with Bunny as she stepped from between two rhododendrons. Fanning away a cloud of smoke, she waved an arm in the air, furtively spritzing an asthma inducing fog of cologne all over herself. And anything unfortunate enough to be within a ten-foot radius. Including me.

"Drugstore knockoff." Darla materialized behind Bunny with a dainty sneeze. Then she opened her mouth, stuck her finger down her throat, and pretended to gag.

"Where are you off to in such a hurry?" Bunny sneered. "Let me guess. Someone called ghostbusters?"

"Busting them isn't my forte." I arched a brow in Darla's general vicinity. "Actually, I'm glad I ran into you. I should apologize."

"Huh?" I couldn't help thinking speechless looked incredibly good on Bunny Bartley.

"Not that you didn't provoke me. Still, I should say I'm sorry." I should, but somehow, I could bring myself to force the actual words past my lips. "Osteomyelitis is a nasty thing, and I wouldn't wish it on anyone, not even you. I'm sure the donor toes will be a great success. In a few months, they'll hardly be noticeable, and your secret is safe with me. So, that's it." It was the best I could do. I stepped around her and hurried along the walk as fast as my unstable heels and wobbly ankles would carry me.

"Why?" Bunny called out behind me. I stopped without turning around.

"Because revenge isn't always sweet, and sinking

your boat isn't the way to make mine more seaworthy."

"Am I supposed to know what you mean?"

I smiled into the darkness. Maybe she'd figure it out eventually. Maybe not. Either way, not my problem. It's never a good idea to wrestle with pigs. You both end up dirty, but only the pig enjoys it. I started walking again.

"It doesn't matter," I called back over my shoulder. "As long as I do. Good-night, Bunny."

I climbed in the car, locked the door, and sat staring into the darkness savoring the peace and quiet. Which lasted approximately one ten-thousandth of a second before Darla popped into the passenger seat, her lips flapping in the wind before she'd achieved full visibility.

"Why on earth would you apologize to that toe-less asshat?" she wailed. "She had it coming. She's always had a thing for Jackson, you know. Not that he's ever given her reason to hope. She acted like a total bitch."

"Let's play a word association game. Pot? Kettle? Black? Any of those resonate with you?" I turned the key in the ignition and shoved the gearshift into reverse. "And I didn't actually apologize, exactly."

"Well, you came damn close. And I am *so* not that girl, anymore." Darla sniffed.

"Only because you're dead. If the Botox hadn't done you in, it would still be you and Bunny, the terrible twosome, business as usual."

"No, it would not. We'd parted ways. Fundamental difference of opinion."

"Let me guess…you couldn't reach a consensus on what color to designate as the new black?"

"Don't be silly. Everyone knows the new black this

season is lime green. No, we never disagreed when it came to fashion. However, I did have a teeny little problem with her tendency to sleep with my husband. I mean, I realize I married the asshat for better or worse, but why should I put up with all the worse, while she sneaked around behind my back hogging what little better he had to offer?"

"Oh, Darla. That sucks. I'm so sorry." And I just missed apologizing to the booty-peddler. What was it Darla said? Hindsight is twenty-twenty. I suppressed an overwhelming urge to turn the car around. It would probably be considered crass to march back into the funeral parlor, drag the faithless wonder to the front of the room, and rip off her red-soled stilettos, exposing her hairy-toed shame to the world. Boy, it was tempting. Keeping one hand on the wheel and one eye on the road, I instinctively reached for Darla's hand. Of course, my fingers passed right through hers, chilling mine to the bone, and denying her even a modicum of comfort.

"Oh, don't be. Harlan Hampton IV is a total dick-wad. I'm just sorry it took me so long to see it."

"Dick-wad or not, betrayal hurts."

"Anyway, I fixed his two-timing ass," she continued as though I hadn't spoken. "He's gambled himself into a hole I'm not sure he'll ever climb out of. No doubt he counted on being back in the black when I conveniently croaked before I had a chance to file for divorce. The look on his face when he discovered I changed the beneficiary on all of my insurance policies was priceless. Honestly, it was almost worth dying for."

"No, it wasn't."

"Okay, not really. But it did make it a little easier

to swallow. Or it least it would have, if my throat hadn't swollen shut."

"What were you thinking? No one needs Botox at twenty-six. Oh sure, maybe if you're suffering from chronic migraines, profuse underarm sweating, or an embarrassingly leaky bladder, but cosmetically? Again, I say, what were you thinking?"

"That I was closer to thirty than twenty and on the verge of ending a marriage to the only man I'd ever been with. Besides, I had a gift certificate for the injections my good-for-nothing-but-misery husband gave me before he knew I planned to dump his ever widening ass. The bastard loved pointing out crow's feet were no girl's best friend. Don't think that didn't rankle when I knew he was screwing bottle-blonde Bunny behind my back. I figured I might as well take advantage of it."

"Who does that?" I frowned as I pulled into the driveway and killed the lights.

"Hey, I had a future to think about. At least, I thought I did. My bad."

"Not you. Harlan."

"Oh, well I'm pretty sure he's a sociopath."

"You don't know what a sociopath is." I tossed my keys on the entryway table along with my small, black clutch. Then I kicked off the heels, scooped them up, and climbed the stairs in stocking feet. Unlike Gran, I ordinarily wore a bra, so my girls weren't protesting overmuch at their confinement. The pantyhose were another story. I was pretty sure the blood flow to any area south of my navel had been non-existent for at least an hour.

"Of course, I do." Darla appeared at the top of the

stairs just as I reached them, and I shivered with the chill of walking through her filmy form. She followed me down the hall to my room and curled up in the window seat as I shimmied out of The Dress, and yanked off the nylon torture device, rejoicing at the immediate return of circulation to my lower extremities.

"Sociopathy is a personality disorder characterized by a complete disregard for anyone's feelings, manipulative behavior, a lack of remorse or shame, and unbridled egocentricity. Furthermore, sociopaths are not only accomplished liars, they are frequently more comfortable with lies than the truth. Check the dictionary. I'll bet there's a picture of Harlan right next to the definition."

I paused in the act of tying the drawstring of my pink, flannel pajama pants and stared, dumbfounded. Who was this ghost, and what had she done with Darla?

"How do you know that?" I sputtered, dragging a tank top over my head. "Big words, accurate description…if memory serves, you barely passed study hall."

Darla waved an airy hand at the built in bookshelves on either side of the window seat.

"As you may recall, for at least a month after I showed up, you did your best to ignore me. I had to do something with my time while waiting for you to acknowledge my existence. I discovered if I concentrated hard enough, I could move objects if they weren't too terribly heavy. And you have a lot of books. I could have gotten an A in study hall like anyone else, you know. I simply had other priorities."

"So, you read my psychology textbook and reached the conclusion Harlan is a sociopath?"

"I believe he suffers from antisocial personality disorder, yes. In fact, I wouldn't be surprised if it was more than my vanity that killed me, after all."

Chapter Nine

"Lucy, I'm home!" Gran sang out in a cheesy Cuban bandleader accent. The woman did love her classic TV. I shoved my feet into my bunny slippers, as Darla inconveniently vanished following her cryptic announcement. Had she just implied her husband had a hand in her untimely demise? I think she did. And just what in the hell did she expect me to do with that?

I pounded down the stairs, stomach churning, head whirling, ears flopping—the bunny slippers', not mine—and skidded to an ungainly halt at the bottom when I realized Gran wasn't alone. Actually, I crashed into Jackson Merritt's back as he helped Gran out of her jacket. Whatever.

"We have to stop meeting like this." He turned and reached out a hand to steady me. I wondered if there would ever come a day when Jackson Merritt would see me at my best—calm, collected, exuding poise. All things considered, it didn't look promising.

"What are you doing here?" That's me, ever the gracious hostess.

"Helen's daughter had car trouble, and Jackson kindly offered to drive us two old ladies home," Gran answered for him. "So, naturally, I invited him in for coffee."

"I hope you don't mind." He offered me a dazzling smile, his thumb absently stroking my bare shoulder.

"Mind?" Just because he still resembled a GQ model and I looked like a dog's breakfast shoved into two fluffy pink rabbits? "Why should I mind?"

"Well, you left in kind of a hurry. I thought maybe I'd offended you."

"If I took offense every time someone made fun of me…well, I'd be offended a lot."

"Who made fun of you? Was it Bunny?" His brows drew together.

"Look, Jackson, I get it not everyone understands what I do. And that's okay. Honestly. Heck, I don't understand it myself. But I refuse to make excuses for something beyond my control. Not anymore. And mocking what you don't understand *isn't* okay. So, if you think you can keep your ridicule to yourself, then by all means, let's sit down and have a nice, friendly cup of coffee."

"Me?" He looked genuinely surprised. "What are you talking about?"

"You said you were hoping for some feedback from Tillie." I lifted my chin and crossed my arms over my chest, shrugging his hand from my shoulder.

"Oh, that." His expression cleared. "I wasn't mocking you, Lucy. It was my apparently lame attempt to let you know the rumors didn't matter to me. I'm sorry if it came across as something else. I really would like to get to know you better."

"Why?"

"What do you mean why? You're attractive, sexy as hell, you're a nurse, so, obviously you're intelligent…" He trailed off and looked down at his feet.

"Keep talking."

Sharon Saracino

"And it's not every woman who can carry off roadkill as footwear." Okay, apparently he'd been looking at *my* feet.

"*Now* you're mocking me." I bit my lip to keep from smiling and tucked one ratty rabbit out of sight behind the other.

"Now I'm mocking you," he agreed with a grin. "In a flirtatious and totally charming manner I hope will induce you to give me a second chance to make a first impression, and get me a cup of coffee."

"Well." I looked at the ceiling, clasped my hands behind my back—all the better to highlight my girls straining against the ribbed fit of my tank top—and pretended to give the matter serious consideration. Frankly, he had me at intelligent. Throw in attractive and sexy, and my hook became close personal friends with my line and sinker. His clear appreciation of my slippers? Simply icing on the cake. "I guess everyone deserves a second chance."

"Lucy, where did you hide the coffee?" Gran called.

"Next to the coffee maker, Gran." I turned and headed for the kitchen, Jackson following close behind. Close enough that I swore I could feel the heat radiating from his body. My lady bits sparked to life in response, clamoring for attention. The confused and slightly fearful expression on Gran's face as she stood at the sink with a coffee filter in each hand doused the flickering flames as effectively as an ice cube down the neck of my blouse. My heart kicked me in the ribs. She'd been so sharp, so lucid earlier this evening. It had been easy to forget the little ways in which she'd begun slipping away.

"Here, Gran." I gently pried the coffee filters from her unresisting fingers. "I'll do it. Why don't you go up and get changed? The girls must be screaming in protest by now, yeah?"

She regarded me blankly for a moment, her gaze shifting to Jackson standing quietly behind me. And then I saw the switch snap on, and the light flare to life in the dark room. She was back.

"Thank you, dear." She patted my cheek. "I should go up and free the poor dears from bondage. In fact, I think maybe I'll just call it a night. Jackson, I hope you'll overlook an old lady's occasional brain cramp. Thank you for the ride."

"My pleasure, Mrs. Ashcroft. And if I run across any old ladies with brain cramps, I promise to turn a blind eye. Lucy, why don't you help your grandmother get settled, and I'll make the coffee?"

"You are a sweet boy. Isn't he a sweet boy, Lucy?"

"He is indeed, Gran." I handed him the filters and hoped my eyes reflected my gratitude at his kindness in minimizing Gran's obvious forgetfulness, thus assuaging her embarrassment. "Coffee is in the canister next to the machine. Mugs are over the sink. Thank you."

I took Gran's arm and led her from the room. Mr. Picklepaw rose from his crouched position on the top of the fridge, arched his back as we passed, then sprang to the floor and followed us up the stairs. He paused in the doorway of Gran's bedroom, licking his paw, while I helped her out of her funeral clothes and dropped her flannel nightgown over her head. While she crawled into bed and I hung her things in the closet, Mr. Picklepaw jumped up and curled in a ball at her feet. He refused to budge, even when I sat down on the edge of the mattress and tucked the covers around her. Seemingly, we'd acquired a permanent pet.

"A mind is a terrible thing to lose," Gran sighed.

"Your mind isn't lost. It's right where it's always been. Little pieces just find it amusing to run and hide from you every now and then. Could happen to anyone. You always manage to find them. Just like your teeth."

"Do you think he noticed?"

"Doubtful," I said, pressing a kiss to her cheek and rising from the side of the bed to head for the door. "I'm pretty sure he was too mesmerized by the sight of my ass in these flannel pants to pay attention to anything as commonplace as an old lady's temporary brain cramp."

"Oh, well, that's all right, then." She smiled and closed her eyes, tugging the blanket to her chin and snuggling down into the pillows. "Spectacular asses run in the family. On my side, of course. You're welcome."

"Goodnight, Gran," I whispered. "I love you." But her soft snores told me she'd already dozed off. A movement in the corner caught my eye. Apparently, Grandpoppy had returned from Uzbekistan and recovered from his jealous snit. He winked and blew me a kiss, settling into the faded armchair in the corner, as I pulled the door closed. Then I remembered Mr. Picklepaw and cracked it open in case the cat suffered from a midnight craving. Or a weak bladder.

I followed the pleasing aroma of dark roast to the kitchen and found Jackson, sans jacket and tie, filling two oversized mugs with fragrant brew. He'd unbuttoned the neck of his shirt, exposing a smattering of crisp, dark hair curling from the base of the open V, and he'd rolled up his sleeves, the bunched fabric snowy white against the tanned skin of his forearms. If I had a view like that in the kitchen on a regular basis, I might actually think about learning to cook. I briefly considered hightailing it back upstairs to change into something that didn't look like I'd slept in it—because I, you know, had—then I decided he'd already seen me, and a girl shouldn't be too obvious. Instead, I slid into the nearest chair and accepted the steaming mug Jackson offered.

"Thanks." I shook my head as he slid the sugar bowl across the table. "I take it black."

"Me too. She okay?" he asked, claiming the chair across the table and taking a sip from his own mug.

"Yeah. She's sleeping. She's a little forgetful sometimes. It's not too bad, at least not yet. But it's hard to see her declining. Harder still that she knows it."

"I can imagine. She's lucky to have you."

"I'm lucky to have her." I shrugged. "I struggled with the idea of coming back here, you know. No one in Florida knew anything about Lucy the Ghost Gabber. Ignorance—other people's ignorance anyway—really can be bliss. But Gran isn't safe on her own anymore. This has been her home for over sixty years. She should be able to stay in it until she dies, if that's what she wants. If people here persist in clinging to the maturity level of preschoolers by their buffed and manicured fingernails, that's their problem." I realized I was babbling and snapped my mouth closed. "Enough about me. Did you always want to be a mortician?"

"It's the family business." He shrugged his shoulders. His wide, magnificent shoulders. "That's why a lot of people make the career choice, I guess. It's not for everyone, but growing up surrounded by death, I accept it's part of the natural course of life. Someone has to guide people through the endless, mundane, and necessary end of life decisions requiring more thought and energy than they're capable of when navigating the worst moments of their lives."

"It can't be easy. I'm sure you help more than you know," I offered.

"I hope so. I do my damnedest to prepare their loved one with dignity and respect, hopefully giving them a last memory of peaceful repose. That can go a long way to mitigate what may have been a difficult passing. My father set a great example in showing me how to help ease the burden of those who grieve."

"That's lovely, Jackson. Truly. I doubt every undertaker cares so much." My gaze was drawn to his shoulders as he shrugged again, straining the seams of the white dress shirt. My attention was then diverted by Mr. Picklepaw as he slinked across the kitchen and disappeared into the laundry room where I'd set up his litter box. Wise decision, leaving Gran's door open a crack. "I think for some people, a job is simply a job. In your case, it sounds like it's more of a calling. I'm sure your clients appreciate it."

"I don't do it for accolades, but it's nice to know something I did made a difference." I'd been referring to his dead clients, but hey, I bet the living were grateful, too. "What about you? Always wanted to be nurse?"

"I don't remember ever wanting to be anything else, so I suppose I did. I never thought I'd be saying this to a funeral director, but I see more than a few parallels in our respective career choices. Challenging, demanding, something people outside the profession will never fully understand. Dealing with people sometimes overwhelmed by their worst nightmare. Hoping to make a difference."

"Exactly." His dark eyes met mine over the rim of his cup and held. If I ever *did* imagine having this conversation with a funeral director, I'd never have imagined Jackson Merritt. Sitting in my kitchen. Drinking my coffee. Looking at me as though I just might be the cherry on his hot fudge sundae. Thankful for the absorptive properties of flannel, I squeezed my thighs together and shifted in my seat.

We chatted through a second cup of coffee about his career and mine, people we'd known in high school, the ways in which Douglasville changed over the years, and the ways it remained the same. Though I hadn't expected it, I felt as though we made a real connection, and the hope I'd tried to ignore bubbled up and percolated in my heart. I suppose all good things must come to an end. A deep growl, followed by a threatening hiss emanating from the doorway of the laundry room had Jackson swiveling his head in that direction.

"Your cat is certainly unhappy about something."

"He's not mine. Well, I guess actually he is. He belonged to Tillie, and it appears Gran adopted him rather than send him to a shelter."

"That was nice of her, though I suspect he'll be more your responsibility than hers." He laughed. "Did you know they say animals can see ghosts, too?"

"I did, actually. Unlike most people, sensing the supernatural is natural for animals because they don't know enough to judge or question it. So, it's probably the big, black lab lying at your feet that has Mr. Picklepaw's nuts in a knot."

"What did you say?" Jackson set his cup slowly and carefully on the table as the color drained from his face.

"I'm sorry. I guess that was a little crass, huh? I just can't get past the fact he's got three of them. Nuts, I mean. I'm not much of a cat person. I wonder if it's a common genetic mutation in felines?" I knew I was babbling again. Why did nuts always seem to insinuate themselves when I engaged in conversation with Jackson Merritt? Oh, yeah, because I kept mentioning them.

"No, I meant about the dog."

"Oh, her. She just appeared a couple of minutes ago and plopped down at your feet. I guess she likes you."

"How do you know it's a she?"

"Pink collar with rhinestones."

"Chloe?" Jackson shot to his feet, sending the chair crashing backward to the floor. The lab's tail rhythmically thwacked the floor as soon as he spoke her name.

"You know her?"

"Yes. No. I mean, she's mine. Uh, was mine. I had her put down three days ago." Jackson raked his fingers through his hair, staring at me wide-eyed as though I'd suddenly turned green. Glancing at his watch, he snagged his jacket from the back of the chair and tossed it over his arm. "Listen, I should get going. Funeral in the morning."

"Sure, I understand." I rose stiffly to my feet.

Funny how he hadn't been in anything resembling a hurry until I mentioned his dead dog. "I have work, anyway. Thanks again for bringing Gran home."

"Uh, my pleasure." He made a wide berth around me as he headed for the front door.

"It's not contagious, you know," I remarked in as casual a tone as I could muster with the tight fist squeezing my heart.

"What?" He turned back in the act of shoving his arms in his jacket.

"Nothing. Goodbye, Jackson."

"See you."

Somehow I doubted it. I locked the door behind him and rested my forehead against it. Maybe if I'd let him get to know me better before shoving the truth down his throat? Of course, then I would have gotten to know *him* better, too, and maybe it would only hurt worse. It didn't help much at the moment. He said the rumors didn't matter and I'd been foolish, or desperate, enough to believe him. Clearly, the rumors didn't matter only as long as the rumors weren't true. While it might be better to find out now rather than later, it still bites when you get your hopes up for fireworks and fanfare, and end up alone in the dark playing a sad, broken kazoo.

Chapter Ten

Rolling out of bed after a relatively sleepless night wasn't nearly as difficult as I anticipated. Dragging my exhausted ass off the floor once I did, however, proved slightly more challenging. I briefly considered sticking an out-of-order sign on my forehead and climbing back under the covers. Gripping the mattress, I heaved myself to my feet, knuckled the lingering vestiges of sleep from my eyes, and looked around. Still no sign of Darla. I don't know why I worried about her. I had enough of my own problems, and realistically, what's the worst that could happen? She already died.

Because there were no full time openings at Good Samaritan when I moved back to Douglasville, I accepted a per diem position. Fortunately, there were always enough holes in the schedule to offer me almost full time hours, and though the position didn't come with benefits, it did offer a higher hourly rate. In addition, it allowed me to pick and choose when I wanted to work. While I did do an occasional evening or night shift if they were desperate for help, I didn't like leaving Gran home alone at night too often. During the day, I dropped her at the Adult Day Care, which cleverly masqueraded as a Senior Citizens Center, assured she'd be safe, well fed, and have fun socializing with her cronies while I worked. And the house would still be standing when I got home.

Gran had the coffee made by the time I jumped in the shower, rinsed off the stink, slicked my hair into a ponytail, and threw my scrubs on. Her wardrobe choice gave me pause. It so closely resembled ordinary, I pressed a palm to her forehead as I passed to check for fever. Cool as a cucumber. I poured a cup of coffee and slid into the chair.

"Is that what you're wearing today?" I raised my brows, while eye-balling her black leggings and a simple, long-sleeved black top. Okay, she was wearing black leather motorcycle boots and spurs, but still.

"I know. It's missing something, right?" She hopped up and came around to my side of the table and held out her hand. "Had trouble with the bustier. My friend, Arthritis is acting up. Old age doesn't come alone, Lucy."

"Turn around." I laughed, lacing her into the gold brocade corset-like apparatus. At least she'd worn something beneath it this time. "Stop sucking in your gut. It'll end up being too tight, and you'll be uncomfortable all day."

"Corsetry isn't worth the discomfort if it doesn't knock at least a few inches off," Darla remarked from the top of the fridge. Mr. Picklepaw promptly joined her and commenced the batting of the boxes. If only the mangy feline reacted as calmly to the ghost of Jackson's dog as he did to Darla, I might have kept from remarking on Chloe long enough to at least get a first date.

"There, how's that?" I tied the ribbons in a bow, and Gran took a deep breath. Then she twisted from left to right and bent forward to touch her toes, making it as far as her knees.

"Perfect."

"Where've you been?" I asked Darla as Gran waddled back to her seat.

"Is it Eugene?" Gran's face lit with a smile. "How was Uzbekistan, dear?"

"No, it's Darla. Grandpoppy dropped by last night. You were already asleep."

"Places to go, people to see, things to do," Darla offered a non-committal response.

"Do these people, places, and things have anything to do with Harlan?"

"Sort of?" Darla frowned. "I don't know. Not him, personally. I hoped to see the woman he had with him at the ED. I swear I know her, but I can't remember from where and it's driving me crazy. Isn't it strange? I can remember almost everything else, even things I did when I was five years old, but I can't place her. Of course, the hour or so preceding my death is still hazy, too, so maybe it'll come back to me eventually."

"Does it really matter who she is? I mean, I know it can't be pleasant to see your husband with another woman, but it isn't the first time, right? And from what little you've told me, I'd hazard a guess he'll be moving on to someone new before long anyway."

"Oh, please. I don't give a rat's ass who Harlan boinks, anymore. There's just something about that woman I feel like I should remember, and I can't."

"What time did Jackson leave, dear?" Gran asked in a voice oozing with innocence.

"Jackson was here? Details, I want details." Darla clapped in glee. "Spill it, ghost girl."

"He was here just long enough for his dead dog to show up, scare the cat, and prove the rumors about me are true. After that, he was in kind of a hurry to leave."

"Well, he did have a funeral early this morning," Gran said.

"So he said."

"Oh, for the love of white shoes after Labor Day, you didn't *tell* him his dead dog was here, did you?" Darla rolled her eyes and crossed her arms over her chest. When she failed to reset the cereal boxes, Mr. Picklepaw attempted to swat her forearm, claws extended. His paw passed right through her, throwing him off balance, and sending him careening to the floor. Following an impressive double somersault with one-and-a-half twists, he landed on all fours, plopped on his ass, and proceeded to groom his left ear as though he'd totally intended to do that.

"Well, excuse me! He said the rumors didn't matter to him. He asked me if Tillie had any feedback. How was I supposed to know he meant the rumors didn't matter only as long as they weren't true? Anyway, it's fine."

"Hmm…problematic, but not hopeless. He's definitely interested. I think you should—"

"I think I should start following my head. My heart is clearly an idiot. Leave it alone, Darla. Please. If he was interested, he isn't anymore. You ready to go, Gran?"

"Just let me get my purse. Have a nice day, Darla." Gran exited the kitchen, waving in every direction except the one where Darla actually hovered.

"You, too, Mrs. Ashcroft," Darla replied automatically. "You don't mean to tell me you're giving up so easily?"

"Darla says same to you, Gran." I called. "You

can't give up something you never had in the first place. There's no point in wasting my time watering things that were never meant to grow. So what are your plans for the day?"

"I haven't decided yet. Whatever they are, they will not involve going to work with you. Firstly, you refuse to wear what I select for you. Secondly, your work consists of sick people, horrid sights, and awful sounds. Thirdly, the aforementioned sick people, horrid sights, and awful sounds also make a girl thankful she can no longer smell. The whole atmosphere is *so* not me. Honestly, I don't know how you do it."

"I'm awesome. Gran, you ready? I'm going to be late." I gulped down my remaining coffee, put both mine and Gran's dirty mugs in the sink, and grabbed my bag. Gran tottered into the kitchen zipping up a large paisley square.

"Ready."

"Gran, where's your purse?"

"Right here." She waved the colorful fabric under my nose.

"That's not your purse. It's the slipcover for the throw pillow from the sofa."

"It *was* the slipcover for the throw pillow from the sofa." She undid the zipper and held it open for my inspection. Hair brush, breath mints, sunglasses, three double A batteries, an alarm clock, and her house keys. "Today, it's my purse. I mean, this outfit just screams for paisley. Accessories are everything, dear."

"Your wallet?"

"In my other purse. Which is not in the microwave—I looked—but, I'm sure it *is* somewhere in the house. Okay, I'm ready." Gran tucked the slipcover under her arm. As I hustled her out to the car, I couldn't help noticing the red in the paisley did show well against the gold bustier. Go figure.

After getting Gran settled at the Senior Center for the day, I raced to the hospital, screeched into the employee lot, and skidded through the automatic doors with forty-seven seconds to spare. It didn't bode well the waiting room already resembled what I imagined last call at The Dollar Bonanza might look like if it had a bar in place of a five-items-or-less checkout line. I slipped through the doors to the treatment area and headed for the locker room to stow my bag and take my last precious breaths of freedom. I could only hope the ED gods were smiling down on me. Then I headed for the nurses' station to get change-of-shift report, which in the ED tended to be short and sweet. Only a few words were needed to convey cases for which we all knew the protocols and treatment plans by heart.

"Ugly. Just plain ugly," Sally Williams, the night shift nurse, warned with a shake of her head as I slid into the chair next to her. "Prepare yourself. You are about to see things. Terrible things."

"Great. Terrible things such as?" I sighed, grabbing a pen and sliding a sheet of paper in front of me. I'd been surprised at the laid-back attitude of the staff considering the parking lot and the waiting room were already filling up. Overall, it appeared relatively quiet, though I would never, ever say so. Every nurse on the planet knows to utter the Q-word aloud is to invite disaster. This is not a superstition or an old wives' tale. It's a well-documented fact.

"An empty coffee pot. We have run out of coffee. It's conceivable you will be required to function without caffeine until Annette from second shift shows up. It's her turn to buy, and she sort of forgot."

"You could have called to warn me, Sal. That's why God invented the drive-thru."

"Indeed. However, I got tied up in room four with a ninety-one-year-old male with a history of bone cancer who's been having left hip pain with weight bearing for *several months*. Mind you, he's seen three different doctors since this pain started. Did he mention it to any of them? Oh, no. Better to wait until two in the morning, call for an ambulance, then whip a half-filled urinal at the nurse who doesn't immediately shoot his ass full of narcotics."

"So, you're blaming an elderly man in excruciating pain for the fact I do not have coffee?"

"No, I'm blaming the quart of pee which required me to waste valuable coffee alert time washing up and changing my clothes. The flinger of bodily fluids has shortening of the left lower extremity with external rotation. X-ray shows a displaced fracture of the proximal femur, probably pathologic. We're waiting for a bed, and ortho and oncology have been consulted. Room two, fifty-three year-old male with chest pain, reproducible to palpation, relieved by Toradol, normal EKG, so likely musculoskeletal. Saline lock in the right hand, flushes without difficulty, labs are cooking. Has a history of hypertension, says he takes his meds…when he can afford them."

"Can we get him some samples to hold him over?"

"Pharmacy is working on it. Room three is a Code Blue who didn't make it, family's been notified, transport is on the way up to take him down to the morgue, and housekeeping knows we need terminal cleaning in there ASAP." Sally pushed back her chair and climbed to her feet with a heartfelt groan. "Bushy is currently sleeping it off in bed one. Friends found him breathing and unresponsive. Blood alcohol was off the charts. Came around with a vengeance. He had a liter of fluids and is now sporting a lovely matched set of four point restraints."

"The guy never learns," I muttered, jotting down the details. Bushy was a frequent flier known to every member of the ED team. Sweet guy when he was sober, a total time suck when he wasn't. "Discharge info ready to go when he wakes up?"

"Yep. And that's all I've got. Fun times with the promise of more to come. You're welcome. The line is already forming, as I'm sure you saw on the way in."

"I *told* you to take down the Free Percocet sign."

Sally raised her hand, palm facing me, and split her fingers into a V. "May the force be with you."

"Wrong movie, Sal. That's the Vulcan sign for live long and prosper."

"I didn't have a lightsaber handy. Sue me. And who could've guessed you were enough of a nerd to know the difference? I am now off for three glorious days, so pick whichever hand gesture you prefer, and rest assured I mean it sincerely. See you next week."

"Enjoy your time off." I stuck my pen in my ponytail, my report sheet in my pocket, and headed back to restock the drawers in my assigned rooms with vomit bags and urine kits before stopping in to check on Bushy. Sleeping like a baby. Well, like a drunk baby snoring loud enough to wake the Code Blue in room three, at any rate.

As the sound of sirens penetrated my

consciousness, and seats in the waiting room became hot commodities, I took comfort in the knowledge recent studies indicate circadian rhythms influence death. Old people are more likely to die in the late morning—specifically eleven a.m.—than at any other time during the day. I squinted at my watch. If I could just make it to lunchtime, maybe things would settle down. Of course, the death at eleven thing only applies to people who've made it to old age. The study had nothing to say about the most common time for all other age groups getting hit by buses, or being bitten by dogs, or getting penises stuck in toasters. Those times appear to be random. At least I found one saving grace in my under-caffeinated day from Hell. My overburdened brain cells remained fully occupied and free from random thoughts of Jackson Merritt all day.

Chapter Eleven

It's a bad sign when I find myself wondering if the week is almost over and it's just started. By the end of my endless shift, I needed to restock the vomit bags twice, had no opportunity to empty my bladder, and my only sustenance consisted of a snack sized bag of stale pretzels consumed between changing an incontinent patient and treating two toddlers for lice. Still, no one died on my watch, so I suppose I could call it a successful shift.

I made it almost halfway to the Senior Center before Darla popped into the passenger seat, startling me into a repeat performance of the jumping out of my skin, and slamming on the brakes reaction. This time I managed to keep the car off the shoulder, but as I glanced over at her with an annoyed frown, the deafening blare of the horn from the oncoming car diverted my attention back to the road just in time to swerve onto the right side of the line. Darla grimaced, and my empty stomach did a spectacular flip. My breath whistled through my teeth as I exhaled in relief at averting the close call.

"You are a terrible driver. I can't believe someone actually thought you were qualified to hold a license."

"I am an excellent driver. You are a pain in the ass."

"Well, if you've been seeing ghosts forever, I don't

understand why you are unable to maintain control of your vehicle every time I drop by."

"Because you don't drop by, you pop in. Without notice. While I'm driving. Most of the phantoms of my acquaintance are slightly less presumptuous."

"Well, I've been waiting all day to talk to you. I mean, you work all day, and then you have to stop at the Senior Center to pick up Gran, and then you'll probably stop for take-out somewhere, because, let's face it, you aren't much of a cook and the old girl has to eat. It takes you *forever* to get home, and you pretty much *are* the only person I have to talk to."

"Oh, my God! Did you feel that?" I gasped, hitting the blinker. I turned into the parking lot of the Senior Center, located in a small strip mall just off Main Street. Gran was outside in front of the entrance surrounded by four old men with canes, two occupied wheelchairs, and a blue haired lady with a rolling walker. Beverly, the center's activity aide, fluttered around the perimeter of the small group, ensuring they all kept to the sidewalk.

"Feel what?"

"I think it might have been the whole world revolving around you. What on earth are they doing?" I unbuckled the seat belt and shoved open the door. "Wait here."

"No more yellow Jell-O!" Gran crowed, pumping a fist in the air.

"No more yellow Jell-O!" Warbled her ardent supporters.

"Gran is clearly a woman on a mission." Darla observed from behind my left shoulder.

"I told you to wait in the car," I muttered without

moving my lips.

"I totally intended to, but my keen sense of social consciousness has been piqued."

I rolled my eyes so hard I almost knocked myself out.

"Hey, Beverly," I greeted the frazzled activity aide. Beverly shoved her wire-rimmed granny glassed further up her nose with the back of one hand, while reaching out to steady Blue Hair's rapidly tipping walker with the other.

"Oh, hi, Lucy. Mrs. Ashcroft, your granddaughter is here," she called over the chanting.

"Hello, dear." Gran wiggled her fingers at me, then turned to address her tribe. "Okay, people, that's all for today. Everyone back inside. We will resume on Thursday after arts and crafts. Assuming management has not met our demands by then."

"Arts and crafts is on Wednesday, Mrs. Ashcroft," Beverly pointed out, herding Gran and her shuffling cohorts inside. I brought up the rear, my forward progress stymied for a moment by the tip of one cane finding purchase on my foot. "Thursday is cookies and yoga."

"Oh, that's all right then," Gran's voice floated back to me. "I guess we'll just play it by ear."

As Beverly assisted the others to comfortable seating, I sidled up to Gran who was retrieving her pillowcase purse from her assigned locker.

"Um, Gran? You *like* yellow Jell-O. What gives?"

"Well, of course I do. I mean, who doesn't? We *all* like yellow Jell-O, dear. We also enjoy green, orange, and red for a change of pace. Neither would the occasional addition of chopped fruit or grated carrots mixed into the stuff go amiss. We're not actually protesting *against* yellow Jell-O so much as demonstrating *for* variety." Gran tucked her paisley pillow pouch under her arm and grinned up at me.

"You realize the center is underwritten by the county? They're sort of restricted by what they get, I think."

"I know, but it isn't about the Jell-O, anyway. Everyone wants to feel needed, Lucy. Some of these folks just sit here all day feeling useless and forgotten. An organized project that does not involve dried macaroni, glue, and glitter gives them a purpose, makes them feel as though they can still make a difference, shake things up a little."

"You are an impressively special little snowflake, you know?" I grinned, looping an arm around her shoulders, giving her a squeeze, and leading her out the door. "Let's go home. How about roast chicken for dinner?"

"You're cooking?" Gran stopped in her tracks, and gazed up at me, aghast.

"When pigs fly. Stopping at the deli."

"Oh, that's all right, then. I wonder if anyone ever stopped to think about all the stuff that's going to happen if pigs ever *do* fly?"

"Can I ask you something?" Darla inquired as I buckled Gran into the passenger seat, relegating Darla to the back.

"Can I stop you?" I muttered as I climbed behind the wheel.

"What's that, dear?" Gran asked.

"Talking to Darla, Gran."

"When you were a kid, did Gran do things like, oh,

I don't know, bake Christmas cookies?"

"Every year." I smiled. "Still does, in fact. Though this year I suspect she might need a little help."

"That's nice. Really, nice. I wish I'd had a grandmother like yours, one that cooked and baked and bought me little presents and spent time with me. Even if yours does wear gold lamé the eighties have sent out a search party for."

"You didn't have a grandmother?"

"Oh, sure I had one, but she didn't do any of those things. She had people for that. I never thought these words would pass my lips. I think I might be a little jealous of you, Lucy Ashcroft."

"Jealous of *me*? You're Darla Swithers, the richest, prettiest, most popular girl in town."

"And you've changed from a mousy little nerd who sees ghosts, to a semi-attractive, smart, grown-up woman who sees ghosts. I admit, I still think it's a little weird, but where would I be if you didn't? You never try to be anything other than what you are no matter what anyone thinks."

"Oh, I tried, I just wasn't very good at it. *Semi*-attractive? Why, thank you, Darla. I'm more flattered than I can say."

"Oh, all right. You're attractive. You've always been attractive. In fact, Harlan thought you were a little *too* attractive, and that's why…" She trailed off into an uncomfortable silence.

"Why you trashed me?" I gasped as all the pieces of the puzzle fell into place. I never understood why Darla felt compelled to single me out and torture someone so far outside her own orbit. What was it she'd said? *It wasn't bullying. I was defending my territory.* "You made me an object of ridicule for the sake of a gambling, womanizing, douchebag who, in your own estimation, is a sociopath, and who treated you like yesterday's leftovers?"

"In my defense, I didn't know he was a gambling, womanizing, douchebag until much later." She sniffed. "In retrospect, I may have made a mistake. We have already discussed the hindsight is twenty-twenty theory. Let's not beat a dead horse."

"I'd rather beat a dead prom queen," I growled through clenched teeth.

"That would be silly. I have no substance, and you would only end up frustrated. However, now I reflect upon it, I think this is really all Harlan's fault. Perhaps you could exact your revenge on him?"

"No, thanks. That would involve interacting with him. I'd rather run naked through Hell wearing gasoline panties." I pulled into the deli and noticed Gran had dozed off. I guess picketing takes a lot out of a person. "Can you stay here and keep Gran company while I run inside and grab a few things?"

"Of course, I can. I'm not incontinent, you know." Darla lifted her chin and crossed her arms over her chest.

"Your bowel and bladder function is not my problem."

"What's that supposed to mean?"

"When you finish reading my psychology text, you might consider perusing the dictionary," I suggested, then closed the door with a gentle click so as not to disturb Gran.

I'd only intended to purchase a rotisserie chicken, a pound of potatoes au gratin, and a can of corn. In other words, dinner for two with the potential for at least one helping of leftovers I could take for lunch. I guess whoever said you shouldn't grocery shop on an empty stomach knew what they were talking about. Thanks to my near starvation, scarcely assuaged by the aforementioned snack sized bag of stale pretzels, by the time I climbed back in the car, I'd not only acquired dinner, I was also the proud owner of aisle three.

Gran continued sawing wood all the way home, while Darla occupied herself poking through the grocery bags, examining my junk food haul and wisely keeping her opinion to herself. She maintained her tight-lipped silence as I pulled into the driveway, roused Gran from her slumber, and schlepped the bags into the house. Perched on the fridge, alternately playing cereal box pick-up and stroking Mr. Picklepaw's head, she remained uncharacteristically mute throughout dinner, failing even to remark on the caloric pitfalls of the triple fudge cake with chocolate syrup I scarfed down for dessert. Finally, when the dishes were washed and put away, and Gran tottered up the stairs to take her bath, I planted my hands on my hips and rounded on Darla.

"What in the name of soft-serve ice cream with sprinkles is your problem?"

"Just looking at that cake will add inches to your hips, you know."

"And there it is. What's up with you tonight?"

She shrugged and drifted down to occupy Gran's abandoned chair. I took up residence in the one across the table and waited.

"I can't shake the feeling there's something I should remember. Something important. It feels like it's right there floating around in front of me like a pesky gnat, and I swat it and swat it, but I miss it every time. It's on my last nerve."

"Maybe you're trying too hard," I suggested. "When I can't remember something, it often pops into my head when I forget about it entirely. Usually when I'm in the shower thinking of nothing more pressing than whether or not I can get one more shave out of my disposable razor."

"Maybe you're right." Darla's expression brightened. "So, in the interest of jogging my memory, let's talk about you and Jackson Merritt, instead."

"That promises to be a very short conversation." I muttered. "Can we please just drop it?"

"Do you honestly expect me to believe you aren't attracted?"

"Attraction is about more than looks, Darla. I hoped you'd have learned that by now. Jackson revealed his true character when he high-tailed it out of here the moment I threatened his concept of reality."

"No, he revealed he found the knowledge his dead dog was following him around unnerving. He loved that dog."

"Yeah, maybe." I knew it had less to do with his dead dog following him around than the fact I could *see* his dead dog following him around. Whatever. "I admit, it's disappointing, but I didn't expect much. Besides, I told you, I came back to Douglasville for Gran, not romance."

"But—"

"Look, I know you feel like you have to make something up to me. You don't. We were kids. Youth is the petri dish of stupidity. So, you don't owe me anything, and you should feel free to move on with a clear conscience whenever you're ready."

"You still want me to leave?" Darla blinked rapidly and her chin trembled.

"I didn't say that. I just want you to know you don't have to stick around to fix anything. Not for me, not for anyone. You're free."

"So you want me to stay?" She sniffed, assuming in a pitifully hopeful expression.

"I didn't say that, either. What I meant is, we're okay and you should do whatever you want to do. Maybe I've unintentionally grown somewhat accustomed to your pasty white face. Still, facts are facts. You're dead, Darla, and you can't just hang around indefinitely."

"Why not?" She crossed her arms over her chest and lifted her chin.

"Well, I don't know. You just can't."

"Oh really? Well, Grandpoppy's been floating around for what, six years? And all those castle ghosts in Europe? Centuries at the very least!"

"That's different. Grandpoppy is waiting for Gran. As for those castle ghosts, given the way most of them died, I guess maybe they have some unfulfilled need for justice or something."

"Well, maybe I do, too. I've been doing some digging. Oh, and I almost forgot. Apparently ghosts can suck the energy from electronic devices and make themselves visible." She nodded enthusiastically. "At least, I can. Also, it's entirely possible I killed your laptop. I am, of course, profoundly remorseful. Anyway, according to my research, allergic reactions to Botox are almost unheard of, especially fatal ones."

"Meaning?"

"Meaning maybe there really was more to my death than meets the eye."

"Darla, you don't still believe Harlan had something to do with it, do you?"

"I guess not." She sighed dramatically, slumping down in her seat. "He's probably not a sociopath, either. But he most definitely *is* a lying, cheating, good-for-nothing ass."

"Still, you must have loved one another once, and being a lying, cheating, good-for-nothing ass doesn't make him a murderer, right?"

"I suppose not. And yes, I did love him once, or thought I did. Is it so wrong to want to blame someone? At least if Harlan *had* been responsible, it would make some sort of warped sense. He wanted his freedom, or he wanted my money. It might make my death a little easier to accept. I can't shake the feeling something else happened to me. No one dies from a simple Botox injection, for heaven's sake!"

"It *is* unusual," I agreed. "But, clearly, someone did."

"I don't want to be dead, Lucy. It isn't fair."

"No, it isn't." I sighed, wishing I had something more profound to offer. "Of course, it's also not fair the weekend isn't three days long and bread makes you fat. I *am* sorry, Darla. I really am."

"Yeah, me too." She looked away. "So, it's okay with you if I stick around for a while?"

"Is that a rhetorical question? Like I have a choice?"

"No. But don't you think it incredibly courteous of me to ask?"

"Incredibly. I guess your mother didn't waste her money on charm school, after all." I attributed the faint twinge in my chest to triple-chocolate-cake-induced acid reflux. It couldn't be a sense of relief she'd decided to stay. We were never friends, and her current transparency rather limited the social potential of her company. Could she be growing on me? Sure, like a rash. "Well, if you're staying around for a while, we need to set some ground rules."

"We do?"

"The bathroom is sacred space."

"Since I technically no longer require bathrooms that seems reasonable."

"No more popping up unexpectedly while I'm driving."

"What if it's an emergency?"

"Such as?"

"Well, how should I know?"

"Boredom does not qualify as an emergency."

"Maybe not in your world." She pushed out her lower lip. I narrowed my eyes and stared her down. She finally rolled her eyes, and threw up her hands. "Fine, I will not appear unannounced in moving vehicles."

"And last but not least, dates, intimate moments, and any and all aspects of my love life are completely off limits."

"Well, I hardly see that as a problem considering you have none of the above." Darla smirked.

"Yeah, well, it could happen," I muttered.

Darla mumbled something under her breath that sounded suspiciously like *when pigs fly*. Since she'd so readily, for her, agreed to my terms, and because I pretty much thought the same thing, I chose to ignore it.

Chapter Twelve

The ground rules remained in effect for all of one hour and ten minutes. Darla disappeared for parts unknown as I tidied up the kitchen and stuck my head through the half open door to check on Gran, who was already snoring peacefully. I blew a kiss to Grandpoppy floating in the corner of her room. Then I gathered up my PJs and headed for the shower. I lathered, scrubbed, exfoliated, and shaved, then simply stood there and allowed the hot water to sluice over my head and down my body in sheets. I could have been content to remain in that position, enjoying the peace and soothing warmth indefinitely. I could have, but the appearance of Darla's grinning face and upper body dissecting the center of my shower curtain shattered my Zen.

"Sacred space! Sacred space!" I sputtered, hunching forward with an arm thrown across my breasts and a hand strategically, if ineffectually, covering my lady parts.

"Oh, did you mean the entire room?" Darla's brows flew into her hairline, and her teeth worried at her lower lip. "I assumed you meant when you were, you know, taking care of business. It's not as if I'd care to be present for that anyway. I mean, eww."

"And you *do* care to be present for my naked hygiene?"

"I hadn't actually thought of it that way, however

as long as I'm here, I feel compelled to mention a bikini wax might be in order."

"Out!" I reached around the shower curtain, groping for the towel, and quickly yanked it around myself.

"But I remembered something."

"I don't care. Out!" I yanked open the plastic curtain with enough force to send Darla's unsuspecting spirit into a backflip across the room and stepped out onto the bathmat with as much dignity as I could muster. Which, at this point, was zero.

"I know why the woman with Harlan seemed so familiar. I remember her now, Lucy. She was there when I died."

"At the hospital?" I frowned, shoving my arms into my robe and gathering it around me over the towel, before letting the sopping fabric fall to the floor beneath. Though my skin remained uncomfortably damp, and water dripped from the ends of my snarled hair, no way would I open myself up to further inspection and unsolicited grooming suggestions.

"No, at the doctor's office. She must be a medical office assistant or something. She prepared the medication and handed the syringes to the doctor. What if it wasn't Botox in those syringes, at all?"

"Don't be ridiculous." My tone clearly communicated my opinion of her amateur sleuthing, but a tiny coil of unease unwound in my stomach. Harlan gave his wife a gift certificate for the injections. Now he appeared to be involved with the woman who worked at that particular office, a woman who'd been assisting when Darla died. Had they been involved before Darla's death? If so, were Darla's outlandish suspicions really so outlandish? And if they did have some basis in fact, what in the hell was *I* supposed to do about it? Darla drifted down to perch on the edge of the tub, while I grabbed another towel and sopped the moisture from my hair. "Okay, what else do you remember?"

"Well, I remember she did *not* have those double D's bouncing around on her chest. They are clearly a recent acquisition or a result of the best push-up bra I've ever seen."

"Let me rephrase the question. What else do you remember that might actually be *relevant*?"

"Oh. Well, let's see." She narrowed her eyes, her brow pleated in concentration. "I remember she seemed quite cordial. Assisted me into the chair and got me settled. Bustled around the room preparing the tray for the doctor, while explaining what to expect and what to do after the injections. Told me when I got home I could apply cool compresses to minimize bruising and swelling, use over the counter products for pain, those sorts of things."

"Seems pretty routine," I observed, tossing the wet towels over the shower curtain rod to dry. "Nothing unusual. Then what?"

"I think they were having a problem with the heat, or maybe I was nervous. At any rate, it was hot as hell in that place. The woman opened a window when I pointed out perspiring does *not* do a body good. Not my body, at any rate. Then the doctor came in and basically repeated what she'd already said, and started the injections. I felt a little pinch, unpleasant, but hardly unbearable. He finished, I felt fine. Before I left, I asked to use the restroom. The heat in *that* little cubicle was worse than in the exam room, so I opened the window in there, too. I took care of business, and while I was washing my hands, I felt a sharp stinging behind my left ear. Almost immediately, my throat tightened and I couldn't breathe. I felt my face swelling until I thought my skin would split. I tried to say something, call out for help, I think, but my tongue filled my whole mouth, and I couldn't get a word out. I yanked the door open, and then everything went dark. It all happened so quickly. I could hear the doctor shouting. His anger came through loud and clear."

"Maybe you heard panic, not anger. Stinging behind your left ear? How odd. Why would you have stinging behind your left ear if you had the injections around your eyes and in your forehead?"

"I don't know." She sighed. "Look, I know I've suggested Harlan had something to do with my death. I didn't mean it. Sure, I grew to despise him, but I've also known him forever. He talks a good game, but he's a coward at heart. Even if he fantasized about it, he'd never be able to go through with it. Unlike Mr. Picklepaw, Harlan doesn't have *any* balls, let alone three."

"I'd rather not discuss Harlan's balls, or lack thereof, if you don't mind," I replied, dragging a brush through my hair. "So, you've finally conceded you were not, in fact, murdered?"

"I've conceded Harlan did not directly cause my demise. I cannot vouch for the boobalicious bimbo. Maybe she saw a golden opportunity to clear a path to Harlan and his money."

"You don't even know if they were together before you died. Besides, Harlan no longer had any money, remember?"

"Well, yes, but it wasn't common knowledge. Seriously, do you not know me at all?"

"My bad. And here I was giving you credit for evolving beyond the appearances-are-everything mentality."

"Oh, I have." She nodded, averting her gaze as I shot her a skeptical look. "Well, mostly. But I hadn't then. I couldn't bear the humiliation of Harlan's failings becoming public knowledge."

"The shortcomings were his, not yours."

"Maybe, but I married him, and if the truth came out, people would have felt sorry for me. At least the ones who didn't cackle with glee. I couldn't bear being pitied or ridiculed. And now I'm dead, the truth *has* come out, and I'm pitied and ridiculed anyway."

"I agree people feel badly, maybe even pity you, now they know what you endured. Especially you dying so young, and in such a bizarre fashion. Don't you think some must admire you, too?"

"Admire me? Ha! The only thing anyone ever admired about me was my uncanny ability to maintain my balance on five inch stilettos under any and all circumstances including gale force winds. It *is* a gift, you know."

"Undoubtedly. However, not every woman is strong enough to literally stand by her man, especially when that man is a gambling, womanizing, douchebag. You did. You kept it all to yourself and protected his reputation, when he didn't deserve it. I'm sure people find that more admirable than pitiful." I didn't strictly believe this applied to the majority of people in town, but surely there must be a few.

"Come on, Lucy. We both know my motives were more selfish than saintly. I did it for myself, not for Harlan." Her lips twisted in a rueful grin. "But thank you for trying."

"You're welcome." I grinned back. "Now float your transparent ass out of here so I can dry off and get dressed."

"Well, you might consider donning a more appealing ensemble than those faded boxer shorts considering Jackson Merritt has been parked out front for the last ten minutes drumming his fingers on the steering wheel, and trying to decide whether to get out and approach the front door."

"What? Why didn't you say something sooner?" I screeched, gathering up my threadbare boxers and rushing out of the bathroom and down the hall to my room. Darla streaked along behind me. "And how do you know he's trying to decide whether to approach the front door?"

"I intended to tell you, honestly. In fact, that's why I came looking for you, but just like you said, as soon as I was in the shower thinking of something else entirely, I remembered where I'd seen the woman. And I know he's trying to decide because, as I told you before, I've always had a keen sense of when someone is arguing with themselves out loud."

"He's talking to himself? About me?" I paused in the act of wriggling my jeans over my still moist hips. "What did he say?"

"Yes, he is, and I am not at liberty to say. Ground rules, remember? Dates, intimate moments, and any and all aspects of your love life are completely off limits." She had the audacity to giggle.

"You had no problem ignoring the ground rules when you crashed my shower."

"I've already explained. I misunderstood the terms."

"Yeah, right. You're impossible."

"I've been called worse. You'd better hurry," she observed, hovering near the window. "He's clearly come to a decision. He's out of the car and heading up the walk. Later, gator."

I yanked up my jeans like a boss and shoved my arms into the sleeves of the nearest blouse in my closet. I hoped Jackson wasn't holding his breath for a clandestine beauty queen at this un-Godly hour. He'd turn so blue he'd give the Smurfs a run for their money. He really could have called first. The fact he might not have my number was a poor excuse. Abandoning the search for my sneakers, I shoved my feet into my ratty bunny slippers—hey, he'd already seen them—and pounded down the stairs while buttoning my shirt. I nearly skidded into the front door just as he rapped lightly on the other side. Not wanting to appear too anxious, I took a deep breath, counted to one, and then flung open the door.

"Hi." Jackson lowered his head and glanced at me through his long, thick lashes.

"What are you doing here?"

"I know it's late. Do you mind if I come in?"

I held the door open, and he stepped inside. Chloe padded right through the wooden barrier behind him and dropped to her haunches at his feet.

"Am I interrupting something?" He looked pointedly at the front of my blouse. I glanced down and saw that in my haste, I'd missed a button or two, leaving the placket gaping and the hem hanging crookedly over the waistband of my jeans. Whatever possessed me to choose a blouse instead of my usual T-shirt? I cleared my throat and spun around, quickly rectifying my unintentional asymmetrical fashion statement. Turning back to face him, I crossed my arms over my chest.

"No. So, what are you doing here? And what's that?"

"A peace offering." He handed me the gift bag that sported a picture of a kitten wearing a birthday hat and holding balloons and gestured toward the sofa. "Do you think we could sit down?"

"I guess." I gripped the bag tightly and followed him into the living room. Waiting until he settled himself on the far side of the couch, I perched on the edge of the cushion in the middle, spine ramrod straight. "And while I appreciate the thought, and the kitten is very cute, my birthday isn't for another two months."

"It's not a birthday gift, but thanks for the heads up." He laughed and draped his arm across the back of the couch behind me. "I told you, it's a peace offering, and the gift bag selection at the Dollar Bonanza is limited. I'm sad to report it's the only store in Douglasville open at this hour. I left in kind of a hurry last night, and I didn't want you to misunderstand. So, I'm here to apologize."

"What exactly did you think I misunderstood? That you said the rumors didn't matter to you or that you ran away screaming like a twelve-year-old girl when you discovered they were true?"

"I don't recall any screaming." He tried an *aw,*

shucks grin. I kept my expression neutral and simply stared back. "Look, I don't blame you for being angry—"

"I'm not angry with you. I'm angry with myself for being a fool who knows better and clearly never learns. Call me a cock-eyed optimist. I dared to believe you were different," I said through stiff lips, carefully avoiding his gaze. "So, maybe disappointed is a better word."

"I readily admit part of the reason I said the rumors didn't matter was I didn't actually believe them. I figured they were just part of Darla's ridiculous smear campaign back when we were kids. I don't—didn't—believe in ghosts. But there was no way you could have known about Chloe, especially the collar. Discovering you actually *could* see the deceased provoked a knee-jerk reaction. I guess I needed a minute."

"You needed a minute? I tell you your dead dog is lying at your feet, you turn green, hop out of your chair, and can't get away from me fast enough. Now you expect me to believe you're perfectly okay with it?"

"Well, sure it sounds bad when you say it like that." He leaned forward and clasped his hands between his knees. "Maybe not perfectly okay. Let's just say I'm working on it. You have to admit it's a lot to swallow, and you've had a lifetime to come to terms with it. I'll probably have questions. And I didn't scream."

"Mental screaming still qualifies."

"Okay, if you're going to kick me out, can I ask you something first?" He sighed and raked his hand through his dark hair.

I pressed my lips together to keep the corners from curling. He had a point. I'd been dealing with this ability my entire life. Was it really fair to expect him to hop on board without time to adjust? Sure, he freaked out, but he came back, right? Bearing gifts. Calling myself every kind of a fool, I decided to give him one more chance. One. I sincerely hoped I wouldn't regret it.

"I'm not going to kick you out. It would be rude, and Gran would lecture me for days. For some unfathomable reason, she likes you. What's the question?"

"Well, I had Chloe for fifteen years. That's a pretty good life span for a large breed. Though I knew she suffered, and it was time, I struggled with the decision to put her down. To discover she's haunting me...I mean, is it something you see often? Maybe she thinks I betrayed her."

"Honestly? I don't see many animals, and I've never actually seen one hanging around their owner like this. If it makes you feel any better, I think it's more likely because she loves you and worries you aren't quite ready to let her go."

"What makes you so sure?" He reached over and covered my hand with his, his expression hopeful, seeking reassurance his dearly departed doggie was okay. Even if he had nothing else to recommend him, what woman could resist a guy who loves an animal so completely? Not this girl. Fully prepared to offer him nothing beyond a cold shoulder when he arrived, my icy intentions underwent a reluctant, and completely involuntary, thaw as the warmth of his skin crept up my arm.

"The big, soulful eyes gazing up at you in adoration, the wagging tail, the lolling tongue, the way she scooches right up against your leg all the time? Pretty sure she's not pissed."

"She's here now?" He sucked in a breath, and mine stuck in my throat.

"Depends."

"On?"

"On whether you intend to take off like someone stuck a tank of nitrous oxide in your trunk if I say yes."

"No." He squeezed my fingers and swallowed audibly. "Not unless you want me to. I mean, c'mon. I spend most of my time up to my elbows in dead bodies, right? It's just I've never had a single experience leading me to believe ghosts exist. Which doesn't mean they don't," he added hurriedly. "Obviously."

"Look, Jackson. I could sit here and tell you I don't see ghosts. I could pretend to be a nice, normal girl you'd be proud to bring home to mother. I'm sure that would make you more comfortable. But if I did, anything between us from this moment forward would be predicated on a lie. So, if you can deal with it, fine. And if you can't, I understand that, too. You wouldn't be the first. I don't intend to take out a billboard and announce it to the world, but I can't—won't—be anyone other than who I am. Believe me, I tried. All the wishing in the world didn't make me the peg that fit the round hole."

"If I didn't think I could deal with it, I wouldn't be here. Which is not to say there won't be an adjustment period. And for the record, I'd have no problem at all taking you home to meet my mother. To be yourself in a world that's constantly trying to make you something else is a pretty impressive accomplishment. Normal is subjective."

Hey, that was my line. "You honestly believe that?" I hardly dared to breathe.

"Yep. So, how does it work, exactly? Do you have to conjure them or something? You know, Ouija boards, séances, cutting the heads off chickens, and dancing naked in the cemetery at midnight."

"I gave up dancing naked in the cemetery when they installed the motion lights."

"Pity." He grinned and leaned back, releasing my hand to drape his arm along the back of the couch again.

"I don't do anything. They just show up. Always have."

"I imagine that can be awkward sometimes."

"Sometimes. Since they're dead and I'm not, I try to cut them some slack." I shifted in my seat until my leg touched his. "Honestly? Most of the reluctantly departed ignore me completely, buzzing around in my periphery like pesky mosquitos, never making contact. Others aren't so good at respecting boundaries. Still, it's my life, and I've never known any other way. I'm used to it, but I probably could have broken it to you a little more tactfully than announcing your dead dog was lying at your feet."

"I'm not sure there *is* a tactful way to break that to a person." Jackson's arm moved subtlety, until it rested across not only the back of the sofa, but my shoulders as well. He shifted closer. I did not find it unpleasant. At all. "So, what do you think? Maybe you work on breaking it to me tactfully when we have, um, company, and I work on restraint? Will it earn me another chance and maybe the opportunity to take you to dinner this weekend? I really would like to see more of you, Lucy, phantom friends and all."

"Well…" I drawled. "I suppose it depends on what's in the bag."

"No pressure there," Jackson muttered, snatching the bag from the floor where I'd deposited it and plunking it on my lap.

"I'm kidding. And you didn't have to get me anything." The fact he'd cared enough about how I might be feeling to come back meant more than any gift ever could. I plucked tentatively at the tissue stuffed on top of the bag. It occurred to me the Merritts were one of the wealthiest families in town. Exactly how badly did Jackson want a second chance? The bag could contain tickets to a show, a Magic Fingers Spa gift certificate, or even—gasp—jewelry! I'd never been a materialistic girl and—not that I'd ever admit it to Darla—I'd had a crush on this guy since the ninth grade. So, honestly it didn't matter what I found inside. Still, my heart skipped a beat, and then began to race as I plunged my hand inside, felt around, and withdrew…

Chapter Thirteen

"A pair of fuzzy elephant slippers?"

"Hey, I'm an observant guy. Your preference for floppy-eared footwear did not go unnoticed, and they were fresh out of bunnies. Hope they fit, I guessed at the size. So, dinner Saturday?"

"Well, sure, now that I've got something to wear." I kicked off my ratty bunnies and slipped my feet into the puffy gray elephants. Then I scooted back on the couch and stuck my legs out in front of me, rotating my feet in every direction so we could both admire the little guys. The ears flopped, the trunks bobbed, and the little plastic eyes swirled in cross-eyed circles. "Perfect."

"Does this mean you're ready to put your poor, sad rabbits out of their misery and give them a proper burial?"

"Frankly." I wrinkled my nose and shoved my bunnies under the coffee table with a newly adorned foot. "I suspect cremation might be the way to go. Fortunately, I know a guy."

"Hmm, well. I'm not licensed for plush animals, so maybe a burn barrel in the backyard?"

"That might be best. Can I ask you something?"

"Sure."

"Why?"

"Why what?" His brows drew together in a puzzled frown.

"Why me? Did someone dare you to ask me out? I bet they did."

His eyes widened, and his brows flew in the opposite direction, then he pressed his lips together and his features tightened. His arm dropped from the back of the sofa, where it had hovered so tantalizingly close to an almost embrace, like he'd been burned, and then he shot to his feet.

"Not lately. Good-night, Lucy."

"What do you mean, not lately?" I scrambled behind him as he stalked from the room. I grabbed the belt loop of his jeans as he reached for the door, and he stopped with his hand on the knob.

"What do you mean, *not lately*?" I repeated.

His hand dropped back to his side, and he turned back to face me, still wearing that tense expression.

"I mean if you'd asked me that question back in high school, the answer would have been yes. Yes, someone dared me to ask you out. I didn't. You want to know why? Because I refused to be part of their game. When they did everything they could to make you miserable, you held your head high and didn't give them the satisfaction of knowing they got to you. I admired that, and always kind of regretted I hadn't gotten to know you better before you and your folks left town. When I ran in to you at the hospital and discovered you'd come back, I realized I had another shot. Here we were, two grown-up, professional people. I figured we'd moved beyond adolescence. Maybe not if you have so little faith in yourself, and such a low opinion of my integrity. You think I'd only ask you out on a dare at this stage of the game? Clearly, you're still wallowing in it."

"Wallowing is such a strong word. I'm happy you thought I carried off the whole they-didn't-get-to-me vibe. Because they did. And while sometimes I dip my toes into those old insecurities, mostly I've decided I like myself just the way I am and don't care what people think anymore. Mostly. It's just with every available Douglasville Deb lined up like your own personal smorgasbord, I don't understand why you'd be interested in *me*." Fudge! That sounded a lot more pathetic spewing out of my mouth than it did rattling around in my head. I looked at my feet and concentrated on wiggling my toes to make the elephant's trunk jump up and down. "I wasn't questioning your integrity. It's just…well, you're Jackson Merritt."

"So my mother tells me." He took a step closer. So close, I swore I could feel his heat right through my clothes. A warm coil of something that might have been desire sparked to life deep in the pit of my stomach. Although it had been so long since I'd had occasion to experience actual desire, I couldn't rule out a spot of indigestion from the triple fudge cake. I risked a glance through my lashes. Nope, it wasn't the cake. Jackson no longer appeared offended. In fact, if anything, he looked amused. "Suffice it to say I've never been much of a buffet guy. Especially buffets consisting of one long, endless selection of vanilla. You remember what I said about vanilla? You, on the other hand—"

"Are the nut." I sighed.

He grinned. "I was going to say the butter pecan."

"A nut is a nut, Jackson."

"Have it your way." He laughed. Then he cleared his throat. "Well, it's late, and I'm sure you have to get up pretty early for work. I probably should be going. Give some thought to where you'd like to go on Saturday."

I hesitated. The danger of falling hard for this guy was real. Seriously, who could resist a man who looked like a demi-god, was haunted by a love-sick dog, and who apologized with fuzzy elephant slippers? All these years I flirted with a rotator cuff injury from patting myself on the back over how well I handled being alone. I convinced myself having lots of friends wasn't as important as having real ones. Except real ones were scarce when I couldn't—or more accurately, wouldn't—completely open up to anyone. Sure, my parents loved me in a cautious, distant sort of way, and of course, I had Gran. My co-workers liked and respected me, but we didn't hang out or share secrets. In reality, I'd been living a half-life. Now the main character in my adolescent and early adulthood fantasies knew the truth, and he hadn't run away screaming. Okay, he kind of had, but he'd come back, right? Only time would tell if he could actually accept the reality of my life as he claimed, or if I'd end up nursing a broken heart. If I never took the chance, I'd never know.

"Actually, I'm off tomorrow. Also, as of four o'clock this afternoon, in addition to the roast chicken I bought Gran for dinner, I am the proud owner of Goldstein's entire snack food aisle, and I'm willing to share. And there just happens to be a Princess Bride movie marathon running on the movie channel tonight."

"Is that an invitation?" He arched a dark brow, and his lips twitched.

"Is that an acceptance?"

"Depends. Will there be popcorn?"

"I think it can be arranged." He reached out and tucked a strand of my still damp hair behind my ear. My stomach somersaulted, in a good way.

"I'm in." I gazed into Jackson's dark eyes and hoped he referred to more than just a spontaneous movie night at the Ashcroft's. My heart kicked me in the ribs, then crept up and lodged in my throat. I haven't yet ruled out accomplishing great things at some point in my life. For tonight, I'd settle for retaining enough composure to avoid dropping the popcorn into my cleavage. It would be a challenge.

"So, uh, I'll make the popcorn." I coughed. "You make yourself comfortable, remote is on top of the TV."

"Sounds like a plan."

"Kettle, buttered, low fat, caramel, or original?" I asked over my shoulder as I headed for the kitchen.

"Your call. Wow, you weren't kidding about the junk food aisle." He called from the living room.

"Let's just say food shopping after an eight-hour shift with little to no sustenance should be illegal."

I tossed a bag of kettle corn in the microwave and splayed a hand against my chest as his low rumble of answering laughter sent my heart racing. The next sound I heard caused it to nearly stop.

"Lucy?" Gran called out. "Who are you talking to? I felt someone in the house. I thought maybe it was nasty Darla again. I don't entirely trust her, Lucy. Leopards don't change their spots."

I raced to the foot of the stairs, as muted pops erupted from the microwave and the mouthwatering scent of freshly popped corn filled the air. I waved

Jackson back into his seat as I hurried past the archway to the living room.

"You probably sensed Grandpoppy. He was here earlier. I'm talking to Jackson, Gran. We were just going to watch a movie. Go on back to bed; everything's fine."

"Oh, that's all right then. Good-night, dear."

"Good-night, Gran," I called back, then turned to face a slack faced Jackson.

"You might want to pick your jaw up from the floor. Otherwise it's going to be difficult to chew your popcorn." I sighed. "Assuming you still plan to stay."

"Your grandmother sees dead people, too?" His Adam's apple bobbed as he snapped his mouth closed and swallowed audibly.

"No, she just senses when they're around."

"I see." He sat down on the sofa. Hard.

"Do you?" I asked softly, as a muted beep sounded from the kitchen.

"Not really," he admitted. "I'm working on it. And yes, I'm staying. I think the popcorn's done."

"Yeah, I should probably get it," I said, walking across the room to perch beside him, instead. "You said earlier you might have questions. I'm thinking right about now, you probably have questions."

"I'm thinking right about now, I could probably use a good, stiff drink."

"Cooking sherry is about the best I can offer."

"You cook?"

"Nope. But every now and then I binge watch the Gourmet Network and am inspired to run to the market and stock up on supplies. It never ends well. Frankly, I've been fantasizing my entire adult life about a man who'll shove me up against a wall, press his body to mine, and whisper in my ear *I can cook.* I think we both know the questions you want to ask have nothing to do with my culinary skills, or lack thereof. So, go ahead, Shoot. Just be sure you're ready for the answers."

"I'm ready." He straightened in his seat. "At least, I think I am. So, your grandfather's been dead for what, six or seven years? And he's still hanging around?"

"Yep. He likes to travel." I risked a tentative smile. "Never had much of a chance when he was alive. And, of course, he watches over Gran."

"Seems reasonable." Jackson nodded, expelling a pent-up breath I don't think he realized he'd been holding. I sure noticed. "They were quite a couple. Makes sense he'd continue to worry about her. And Darla?"

"Well, Darla has been the white to my rice for the last six months. As you might imagine, she's having a little trouble accepting her situation."

"I suppose she would. We pretty much grew up together, you know. I knew her as well as anyone, and maybe better than most. I didn't agree with some of the things she did and wasn't shy about saying so, but she wasn't naturally mean. Most of the nasty things she did were rooted in insecurity."

"Yeah, I've pretty much picked up on that. Who knew? She said you told her to stop trying to build her happiness on someone else's misery. Meaning mine. You defended me without knowing me." I laid a hand on his thigh and squeezed.

"I didn't have to know you. I knew Darla. Her desperation to maintain her position as the first link in the social food chain and keep her claws firmly embedded in Harlan Hampton IV colored every action. The guy wasn't worth the shot and powder to blow his head off. She thought being Mrs. HH IV would make her happy. Couldn't change her mind no matter what I said."

"You liked her, didn't you? The real Darla, I mean. The one she hid from everyone else."

"Yeah, I did. I wish she could have seen the good qualities, the potential, I saw. Maybe she'd have been happier. Maybe she'd have done things differently."

"I'm glad you liked her. She deserved someone who cared about her despite having nothing to gain."

"She did." He covered my hand with his. "Though I'm surprised you, of all people, feel that way. And a tragic and untimely death doesn't give her the right to go on tormenting you from the afterlife."

"Oh, she's not tormenting me. She's sucking up." I patted his thigh—his hard, muscular thigh—smiled, and rose to my feet. Halfway across the room I turned to regard Jackson's perplexed expression. "I'm pretty sure she also half believes someone murdered her. So, what'll it be with your popcorn…water, cola, or cooking sherry?"

"What do you mean she thinks someone murdered her?" Jackson stalked into the kitchen right behind me, grabbed my arm, and spun me around, trapping me between him and the counter. "She had an allergic reaction. How does she spin that into a crime?"

"Who?" All rational thought fled. My girly bits jumped to attention and quivered in response to the full length of Jackson's body pressed against mine.

"What?" Jackson gasped. Dare I hope he felt similarly affected? Um, yay! He gazed into my eyes, and then lowered his head. My lips parted in anticipation as though they had a mind of their own. Hopefully, they did, since mine had currently turned to mush. He touched his mouth to mine, ever so briefly, and then grazed his lips along my cheek, feathering whisper soft kisses from the corner of my mouth to the lobe of my ear. The open popcorn bag slipped from my numb fingers, scattering kernels across the kitchen floor. Sensing an unanticipated treat, Mr. Picklepaw sprang into action, jumping down from the top of the fridge. That cat was really the best vacuum I'd ever owned.

I allowed my head to fall back, giving Jackson better access, and I fisted my hands in the front of his shirt. When he ran the tip of his tongue around the curve of my ear, my knees threatened to give out. And then it happened. His warm, moist breath ruffled my hair and heated the sensitive skin on the side of my neck as he whispered, "I can cook."

Chapter Fourteen

Jackson captured my lips. He took his time, giving me a slow, exquisitely gentle kiss. His tongue dueled with mine, enticing and teasing, and my train of thought derailed completely. Good gravy, the man's mouth should be registered as a lethal weapon.

"You can cook?" I stammered, when he lifted his head at last. Because I, you know, am all about bringing the sexy.

"Like a boss. And you can sure as hell kiss." He sighed, tucking a wayward strand of hair behind my ear. "Also like a boss, in case you were wondering. Now, explain to me what makes Darla believe she was murdered."

"I said she half believes it," I breathed, struggling to concentrate on the conversation and ignore the spine-tingling sensation of Jackson's finger tracing the line of my throat. "She does have a tendency to waffle in her convictions. Frankly, I think she just needs someone to blame. I mean, sure, an anaphylactic reaction to Botox is rare, but it happens. And just because Harlan gave her a gift certificate for the injections, and the woman with whom he is currently dancing the horizontal mambo happened to be assisting the doctor when Darla died, it doesn't add up to a conspiracy. It's a coincidence, right?"

His eyes widened, and a long breath whistled

through his teeth. His arms tightened around me imperceptibly.

"Right. I mean, I know Harlan needed money, but I've known *him* since we were kids, too. The guy doesn't have the guts or the stomach for murder. Though he talks a good game, he's a spineless coward at heart."

"That's what Darla said. I believe she may have referenced a lack of balls. Which makes sense, really. I recently read a study about howler monkeys which explains it nicely."

"Howler monkeys?" He didn't even have the decency to hide his amusement.

"Yes, howler monkeys. They may be small, but they have one of the loudest and most intimidating calls in nature. Kind of like a loud angry bull trapped in a fifty-gallon oil drum."

"I may regret asking." He rested his forehead against mine. "In fact, I'm ninety-nine point five percent sure I'll regret asking. What do howler monkeys have to do with Harlan's balls?"

"Well, there were these researchers who conducted volume measurements on the testes of howler monkeys." I couldn't believe I'd interjected the subject of balls into yet another conversation with Jackson Merritt. Of course, this time I could quote scientific research. "They also analyzed the monkey's calls, and measured the size of their hyoid, a bone in the throat that amplifies the calls. They discovered the bigger the hyoid, the deeper, louder, and more menacing the particular animal's call."

"So, let's see if I've got this straight." He grinned. "Big hyoid, loud mouth, total badass. Macho monkey?"

"You'd think." I grinned back, tentatively slipping my arms around his waist. "As it turns out, the study also determined the bigger the hyoid, and the louder and more vocal the animal, the smaller the testes. In conclusion, I give you, Harlan Hampton IV. Big mouth, little balls, total wimp. Science doesn't lie."

His eyes widened, then his body shook with a gusty laugh.

"Well, that explains a lot. Trust me, Harlan didn't have anything to do with Darla's demise. And though she may work for the doctor, I doubt his current hoochie mama possesses the brains to carry off any kind of successful scheme. Besides, Doc Monroe did the autopsy, and his findings were consistent with an anaphylactic reaction. Tragic, but true."

"How did you know Harlan had a hoochie mama?"

"Told you, I've known Harlan a long time. Darla was the only classy woman he ever had the good sense to become involved with."

"That's the sweetest thing anyone's said about me since I died." Darla sniffled, wrapping her transparent arms around Jackson and snuggling up against his back.

I stiffened and pressed my lips together as Jackson shivered and narrowed his eyes. "Lucy, is there anything you'd like to share with me at this particular moment in time?"

"Tactfully?"

"If possible."

"Well, I'll give it a shot. Um, the reason your back feels icy cold is because your front is pressed against a smoking hot chick. It's all about contrast."

"Actually, that's not bad."

"So, you'll buy it?"

"Not a chance, though I do appreciate the effort. We have company, don't we?"

"I'm afraid so." I sighed. "You remember when I told you some spirits have a problem respecting boundaries? Some also have a teeny little issue observing ground rules." I glared over his shoulder at Darla, whereupon she released my man candy and glided toward her perch on the fridge. "And have extraordinarily sucky timing."

"Who knew he'd still be here? I am pleasantly surprised, and half-heartedly impressed, by your unforeseen prowess." Darla frowned. "What in the name of strawberry lip gloss are you wearing on your feet?"

"My new elephant slippers. They are cute, cuddly, and comfy. They are a gift from Jackson. I love them."

"Darla?" Jackson whispered, glancing furtively over his shoulder.

"How many other ghosts do you think require me to defend my footwear choices?" Well, I hadn't had to justify them to any other ghosts *recently*.

"Point taken. So, is she gone?" He mumbled without moving his lips. "I'm not cold anymore."

"No, she's on top of the fridge. She isn't touching you anymore. That's why you aren't cold."

"I see." The expression, and sickly pallor, on his face said otherwise. "She touched me?"

"Hugged you, actually. She's deeply moved you consider her a classy woman. Are you okay?"

"Yeah. Yeah, I'm fine." He shook his head as though to clear it. "Actually, it's not the first time I've felt something like that. Occasionally, when I'm down in the basement, preparing a client...well, there are these cold spots. I never really thought much about it before, but now…" His dark brows flew up to his hairline as his widened eyes locked on mine. "You don't think—"

"It's an old house, Jackson. Maybe you need a new heating system."

"I had the entire HVAC redone last year."

"Drafty windows?"

"New windows, insulation, and weatherproofing."

"Would you like me to have a look?"

"They don't stay," Darla offered. "They're simply curious. They want to see what happens to their bodies after they leave them. Then they move on."

"How do you know?" I directed my question over Jackson's shoulder. Darla rolled her eyes so hard she almost knocked herself off the fridge. "Oh, yeah. Duh."

"What?" Keeping one arm around me, Jackson turned and squinted across the room at the fridge as though doing so might enable him to see what I did.

"Darla says your place isn't haunted. Spirits drop by to see what you're doing with their mortal remains. They don't stay."

"I see," he said again.

"You say that a lot." I laughed.

"Only when I'm around you." He smiled and squeezed me against his side. "Give a guy a break, Lucy. It's a lot to process. I'm working on it. Obviously, I don't have a problem with the dead, or I couldn't do what I do. Although, I didn't believe in ghosts, until now. Bottom line is I still think the living are the ones you have to worry about. They do a lot more damage."

"See, I told you he was perfect for you." Darla's

lips stretched in a garish grin.

"Can you give Darla a message for me?" Jackson asked.

"Can you give *Jackson* a message for *me*?" Darla snapped. "I'm dead, not deaf. By the way, maybe you could share the information with Gran, too. Good Lord, that woman is loud."

"Darla says she can hear you just fine." I coughed, covering my mouth to hide a grin.

"Oh, okay." He cleared his throat, then leaned down next to my ear and whispered. "Where is she, exactly?"

"Top of the fridge," I whispered back, suppressing a shiver as his hot breath warmed my neck. He straightened and fixed his attention on Gran's olive green, overdue for replacement appliance.

"I feel a little silly talking to a refrigerator," Jackson confided quietly. Then he straightened and cleared his throat. "Okay, here goes. Darla, perseverating on your death doesn't change it. You need to accept it and move on."

"Oh-Em-Gee!" Darla gasped, a filmy hand fluttering at her throat. Her face crumpled. "I thought we were friends. He wants to get rid of me."

"Don't get your thong in a knot, Darla. I'm sure he didn't mean it the way it sounded." I leaned into Jackson and stage whispered from the side of my mouth. "She thinks you want her to leave. Permanently."

"I do." He nodded. I could barely discern his explanation over the pitiful wails emanating from the top of the fridge. "I mean, I know things didn't work out the way she hoped during her lifetime. I understand she's angry and upset to find herself deceased. But clinging to a life she no longer has can't be healthy, right?"

"No idea," I replied, resisting the urge to clamp my hands over my ears and drown out the ear-splitting howls bouncing around the kitchen.

"Darla, you know you made some half-assed decisions when you were alive. Now's your chance to change the pattern and do what's best for *you*. I wish someone could undo what happened. We all know that's not possible. Move on and find peace. You deserve it. Maybe more than anyone I know."

Darla's trap snapped shut, and the pathetic cacophony ceased with an abruptness that left my ears ringing. Her brows rose into her hairline, and she crossed her arms over her chest.

Why, bless your heart, Jackson Merritt," she sniffled with a smirk.

"She said 'bless your heart'." I squeezed Jackson's trim waist and smiled, absently wondering why her sentiment didn't quite match her expression.

"Oh, she did, did she?" Jackson's brows slammed together, and his expression darkened like a thundercloud. His arm dropped from my shoulders, and he planted his fists on his hips, his feet spread shoulder-width apart like someone prepared for battle.

"Isn't that a good thing?"

"Apparently you're unaware *bless your heart* is Darla-speak for *you're a flipping ass-monkey*," Jackson growled. How was I supposed to know? I took Spanish in high school.

"I'm sure she didn't mean it that way. In fact, I think you made her feel better," I soothed, sure of nothing of the kind.

"Of course, he did." Darla grimaced. "Someone I loved like the brother-I-never-had confirms I made lousy decisions in life, and clearly desires my immediate absence in death. How could I not feel better?"

"She said she loved you like a brother." I conveniently ignored the rest, desperate to diffuse the escalating tension before the entire evening deteriorated from potentially hot-and-schmexy to Night of the Annoying Dead.

"She did?" Jackson's tense expression eased. His fingers slowly unclenched, and then he released a breath, and looped an arm around my shoulders again. "I loved her, too. And while it's comforting to know she continues to exist somewhere, it shouldn't be here. I'll miss her, but she deserves to find the happiness that always eluded her. That'll never happen if she continues to hang around mourning what could have been, and bemoaning things that can't be changed. That's all I'm saying."

Darla drifted down from her perch on a long, drawn out, and overly dramatic sigh. "Need I elaborate how absolutely maddening it is to admit he's right? Please don't feel compelled to communicate that little tidbit. Trust me, he knows."

"She says you're right," I smirked.

"You have a very big mouth, Lucy the Ghost Gabber." Darla frowned, twirling a lock of shiny blonde hair around her index finger.

"And you look like a five and a half foot Easter egg in that purple velour," I shot back.

"Purple velour?" Jackson's mouth dropped open.

"No, no, no. She hated that track suit. I dressed her in lime green shantung silk. It's the new black, you know."

"I heard." I laughed. "And I bet you made her look absolutely beautiful. However, when it comes to the afterlife, it's been my experience if you don it and die, whatever you're wearing becomes your fashion statement for all eternity."

"That's plain sad." Jackson shook his head. "Of course, it could be worse. She could have died while taking a shower. Wet hair, bare-faced, and bare-assed."

"I know, right?" Darla concurred. "On the upside, at least I'm not wearing stuffed animals. You'd best reconsider your footwear choices, girlfriend."

"I'll worry about my footwear. You worry about being mistaken for Barney. Jackson and I were just about to watch a movie. Since you are currently in clear violation of ground rule number three, why don't you pretend you're a ghost and disappear?" I waved my hand at her in a shooing gesture.

"Oh, you are *so* funny I forgot to laugh." Darla stuck out her tongue and dissipated.

"She's gone." I grinned, stepping out of Jackson's arms and grabbing the dustpan from a hook on the wall behind the laundry room door. He courteously stepped clear of the scattered kernels as I swept up Mr. Picklepaw's leftovers, dumped everything into the abandoned popcorn bag, and dropped the whole mess in the trash.

"You mean she actually listened to me for a change?"

"Oh, hell no! She'll be back. But not for a couple of hours."

"Then I guess I'd better take full advantage of the time I've got." Jackson hauled me against his solid form, pinning me between him and the counter. Heat pooled in my stomach, and my thighs quivered as he traced my bottom lip with the tip of his tongue. He captured my mouth and dipped inside. Then he withdrew and plunged again, over and over, mimicking a rhythm as old as time. My lady bits wept with joy and pulsed in time to his music. They've always been percussion groupies.

"How committed are you to watching that movie?" Jackson panted against my lips, his dark eyes drowsy with passion.

Movie? I blinked. *What movie?*

Chapter Fifteen

"Lucy," an urgent voice hissed in my ear. "Wake up! You're drooling."

I cracked a lid wondering why my pillow felt much firmer than usual, and furry, and so incredibly warm. Then I realized it wasn't my pillow. I jack-knifed to a sitting position and dragged my sleeve across my mouth, successfully capturing a trickle of spittle that came perilously close to plopping onto Jackson's bare chest.

"Thanks."

"That must have been one hell of a movie." Darla smirked, her eyes roving over Jackson's half-buttoned shirt and my general state of dishevelment.

"Let's just say I wouldn't mind seeing it again."

"Wouldn't mind seeing what again?" Jackson yawned. He stretched his arms over his head with a groan, his chest muscles rippling, and tossed Gran's afghan on the back of the sofa. I scooted to the end of the couch, and he swung his legs over the side and sat up.

"Um, Darla asked how we liked the movie."

"Oh, it was definitely worth seeing again." He winked. I sighed. Darla cackled. "In fact, it's my new favorite." He reached out to tuck a strand of hair behind my ear, then leaned in for a soft kiss. I pulled back when he would have deepened it. Hey, I hadn't brushed my teeth yet. Can we spell morning breath?

"Coffee?" I climbed to my feet and stretched. Then I grabbed the remote and clicked off the TV.

"What time is it, anyway?" Jackson asked, squinting at his watch.

"Well, good morning, you two," Gran sang from the bottom of the stairs. "Enjoy the movie?"

"Time for Gran to get up, apparently," I muttered apologetically. "Morning, Gran."

"Morning, Mrs. Ashcroft." Jackson tugged his shirt together and buttoned up, before jumping to his feet and tucking it into his jeans. "Sleep well?"

"Like an old man in a hot church on Sunday," Gran assured him with a big grin. She teetered down the hall to the kitchen. "You kids relax. I'll make the coffee. Lucy, your bra is under the end table if you're looking for it. 'Course you probably knew that. Haven't found my wallet yet though, so maybe you could keep an eye open for it while you're crawling around down there?"

"Sure, Gran." I sighed, warmth creeping into my face as Jackson chuckled under his breath.

"Her wallet's in the breadbox behind the English muffins," Darla offered helpfully, before zipping off to join Gran.

I climbed to my feet after successfully snagging my discarded brassiere and tossing it on the sofa. Jackson gathered me into his arms and rested his chin on my head. It had been ages since I spent the entire night with a man—a living one at any rate—and never one who'd captured my heart as quickly and completely as Jackson Merritt. I hated to see it end.

"Listen, I should probably get going," Jackson said. "I have a pre-planning appointment at nine-thirty.

It's already seven and I need to be showered, shaved, and suited up."

"Pre-planning?"

"Yeah. Some folks prefer to choose everything themselves and pay for it in advance. Then when the time comes, there's no burden on the family. All the arrangements are already made."

"Sure, okay. You want a coffee to go? I have four thousand, three hundred and twenty-seven travel mugs. I think I can spare one, even if you…" I cleared my throat. "Never get around to bringing it back."

He placed his hands on either side of my head and tilted my face up. I kept my attention stubbornly riveted on the top button of his shirt. I didn't want to look into his eyes and know he would never get around to it. That there would be no dinner date on Saturday. That we'd shared one almost magical night, and now his curiosity about Lucy the Ghost Gabber had been satisfied. I'd been down this road before.

"Lucy, look at me."

I took a deep breath, blew it out, and raised my gaze to his.

"Seeing you have four thousand, three hundred and twenty-seven travel mugs, I doubt you'll miss one, even if I never return it. Of course, since I *don't* have four thousand three hundred and twenty-seven—in fact, I'm not sure I have *one*—maybe I should hang on to it so when we watch a movie at my place, I can return the favor."

"So, you're saying there will be more movie nights?" I asked, struggling to maintain a deliberately casual tone. The rattle of my elephant slipper's eyes as I discreetly happy-danced in place may have negated the whole   doesn't-matter-to-me-one-way-or-the-other effect.

"Movie nights, dinners, baseball games. I can't believe you need to ask. Unless you don't want..." He trailed off uncertainly.

"No, I do! Of course, I do. I just thought maybe after last night...I mean, it's not that I didn't want to. But we haven't even had a date yet." I smiled and slipped from his arms.

"I think I should be insulted you even considered the possibility I was *that* guy. It's not how I roll, Lucy Ashcroft."

"I didn't think you were that guy." At least, I'd hoped not. "Let me grab the paper from the porch, and we'll get your coffee to go."

I yanked open the front door, delighted to discover the paper boy actually managed to lob the morning edition as far as the top step. Most days, I needed to hike halfway down the front walk in order to peruse the current events in my little town. I bent to seize the rubber-banded bundle, hoping Jackson went ahead into the kitchen and was not behind me observing this awkward squat. As I straightened, a movement at Tillie's place caught my eye.

"What the hell is *he* doing here?" I muttered, squinting across the street.

"Who?" Jackson asked, pushing open the screen door to let me back into the house. So, my ungainly newspaper retrieval skills had not gone unnoticed.

"Harlan. He's skulking around Tillie's house and peeking in the windows."

"Probably calculating how much he can get for the place. The will is being read later this morning."

Jackson shrugged.

I tossed the paper on the hall table. I grinned and grabbed Jackson's hand. "Well, that should be fun. Be right back, Gran," I called, dragging Jackson out the door.

"What are you doing?" he asked, as I dragged him across the street.

"Saying hello to Harlan."

"You don't like Harlan."

"I don't like a lot of people. It's no excuse for rudeness. Hey, Harlan," I called pleasantly, while approaching the porch. "What's going on?"

Harlan Hampton IV, with a yellow legal pad tucked under his arm, peered into the front window, hands cupped on either side of his face, nose pressed against the glass. He started at the sound of my voice, and jumped away guiltily.

"Jackson? What are you doing here? And who...*Lucy Ashcroft*?" He tugged a handkerchief from his back pocket and mopped his brow. "I heard you were back in town."

"And I heard about Darla. I'm so sorry for your loss, Harlan." And I *was* sorry about Darla. For her sake, not his. My eyes took a discreet inventory, shocked by what I saw. The years had not been kind to Harlan Hampton IV. The once muscular physique gone to fat, clothes rumpled, eyes bloodshot in a bulbous-nosed, puffy face. Harlan, the rich kid, star athlete, Prom King, who thrived on being a big fish in a little pond. Apparently he hadn't fared well once high school ended and he found himself a little fish floundering in a lake.

"Who'd have thought, huh?" He sighed. "We had

our differences, Darla and me, but she didn't deserve to die that way."

"She didn't deserve a lot of things," Jackson countered evenly, squeezing my fingers. "So, what are you doing here?"

"Just having a look around. The will is being read this morning. Tillie never had a family, and me being her godson, well…" His voice trailed off.

"You figure you'll inherit it all," I finished for him. "So, you dropped by to tally up the potential haul."

"Seems reasonable to assume." He shrugged.

"Careful, Harlan. You know what they say about people who assume. What about the cat?" I asked.

"The cat?"

"Surely you remember Mr. Picklepaw? Tillie loved that cat."

"Oh him." Harlan's lips twisted in distaste. "Had no idea the mangy thing was still alive. Drop it at the shelter, I guess. I mean, do I look like a cat person?"

"Actually, I'd wager you have more in common with a howler monkey," Jackson offered with a grin.

"What?"

"Nothing." I jammed an elbow into Jackson's side, choking on the effort it took to swallow the giggles. "So, anyway, Harlan, my gran's been taking care of Mr. Picklepaw since Tillie passed. To tell you the truth, she's grown kind of fond of the little guy. If you've no plans to adopt him yourself, would you consider letting her keep him?"

"Fine by me." Harlan shrugged. "He isn't worth anything, and it's one less pain in my ass."

"Can I have it in writing?" I nodded at the legal pad absorbing the profuse perspiration under his arm.

"Seriously?" Harlan's eyes widened and I felt, more than saw, Jackson's puzzled expression. "It's a mangy, useless cat with one foot in the grave."

"He also has three balls, but that is neither here nor there. I don't want you breaking Gran's heart if you change your mind," I said, tugging at the moist tablet. I released Jackson's fingers and held out my hand for the pen.

"I, Harlan Hampton IV, being of sound mind," I recited aloud as I wrote. I paused and looked Harlan up and down. "And a body that's seen better days, hereby relinquish all rights and claims, now and in perpetuity, to Mr. Picklepaw, elderly three-balled orange tomcat, and the beloved pet of my godmother, the late Tillie Colton. My signature below indicates I have no interest in the aforementioned feline, and agree that possession and ownership of said cat should be assumed by Lucy and Beulah Ashcroft immediately upon the death of Tillie Colton, in the best interest of the animal."

I finished with a flourish, and handed the pad to Harlan. "Sign and date, please."

He snatched it from my fingers with an eye roll worthy of yours truly, and scratched his signature at the bottom.

"Darla was right about you," he grumbled, shoving the tablet at me. "You're nuts."

Wordlessly, I added my own signature as witness, and handed the pad to Jackson. My heart tripped happily when he never questioned it, and simply scribbled his name below mine. I tore off the sheet, folded it, and stuffed it in the back pocket of my jeans.

"Thanks, Harlan." I smiled and reached for Jackson's hand. "I sure hope you don't regret passing up the chance to have Mr. Picklepaw for your very own."

"I won't," he grumbled.

"Oh, somehow I think you might," I muttered under my breath. Waiting until we descended the porch steps and were halfway along the front walk, I tugged Jackson to a stop, and turned. "Darla was right about you, too, Harlan. You're a lying, cheating, good-for-nothing ass. Still, I'm pretty sure she's wrong about you being her murderer. Have a fabulous day, and good luck with the will."

"What exactly was that all about?" Jackson asked, snatching the newspaper from the hall table and trailing me into the kitchen.

"Just protecting Gran's interests." I smiled, filling a travel mug with coffee. I handed it over, my fingers lingering as they touched his. "She's gotten quite attached to Mr. Picklepaw. I don't want Harlan getting any ideas about trying to claim him." I patted my butt, and tugged the paper from my pocket. "Thanks for playing along without questions."

"No problem. But I doubt you needed it in writing. Harlan has zero interest in the cat beyond how much of a time suck it'll be to drop the poor thing at the shelter," Jackson observed, raising the cup to his lips.

"That may be true at the moment. Somehow I suspect he'll be an avid animal lover once the will is read."

Jackson lowered his coffee, eyes wide. "No, she didn't!"

"Oh, yes she did," I confirmed with a wink. As though he understood he was the topic of conversation, Mr. Picklepaw chose that precise moment to strut into the kitchen, tail hoisted proudly in the air, overburdened ball-sack swinging like a pendulum. He pranced across the linoleum, sprang onto Gran's lap, and promptly started snoring.

"Lady and gentleman." I raised my coffee mug in the direction of the oblivious mouser. "I give you Mr. Picklepaw, soon-to-be the wealthiest cat in Douglasville."

Chapter Sixteen

"How did I not know you were a tramp?" Darla pondered from her perch atop the fridge.

"Um, because I'm not?" I plunked the plate of orange mac and cheese mixed with sliced hot dogs in front of Gran and stepped back to the stove to ladle out a hefty portion for myself. It might not be the most nutritious entrée, but it's something I can actually cook, and it's what Gran requested. I figure, at her age, she should get to eat whatever she likes. Besides, her dentures were on the lam again, so soft food seemed like a safer bet.

"Don't get me wrong, Jackson Merritt is delicious. What girl wouldn't want to sink her teeth into a piece of that? Well, except for Gran, who can't actually find hers. They're in the cookie jar, by the way. Don't worry, she ate the rest of the cookies first," Darla added when I gagged a little. "Don't you think you should have held out for an actual date first?" She drifted down to take a seat at the table. I wanted to be annoyed we were discussing this at all, but the fact she respected the ground rules and held her tongue in the matter of my love life all morning, right up until lunch time, persuaded me to have a little tolerance.

Noting Darla's avid interest in my food, I shoveled a forkful of orange pasta and frank bits into my mouth, moaning with the rapturous appreciation of someone indulging in the finest cuisine ever plopped on a plate. I figured out a long time ago just because ghosts *can't* eat doesn't mean they don't want to, especially since they no longer needed to worry about dietary restrictions or weight gain. My tease produced the desired effect. Darla licked her lips, swallowed hard, and looked away. Callous of me, perhaps, but she had pretty much just called me a woman of questionable virtue.

"If you continue bashing my morals, I swear I'll have a banana split for dessert," I threatened, jabbing my fork in her direction. "With extra whipped cream and three cherries."

"That will be far more detrimental to your hips than to mine." Darla sniffed.

"Jackson and I have a dinner date on Saturday, if you must know," I snipped right back.

"Not at the Country Club, I hope?" Gran asked with a shudder. "Bad juju in that place, if you ask me."

"I didn't ask, but your observation is duly noted," I said, turning my attention back to Darla. "Besides, nothing happened. Well, not *nothing* exactly, but not *something* either, if you get my drift."

"Oh, I get your drift, dear," Gran mumbled through a mouthful of macaroni. "And I can see how *some* people might construe the brassiere under the table as incriminating. I, on the other hand, am an ardent proponent of allowing the girls free reign, especially at bedtime."

"Exactly." I knew sleeping without a bra permitted the gravitational pull of my breasts on their supporting structures. This, of course, would eventually result in Cooper's Droop—lengthening of the ligaments which keep the ta-tas perky. Gran had been the poster child for years, and could, in fact, tuck her bosoms into the waistband of her pants when she allowed them to hang unfettered. I'm a nurse, and therefore sleep deprived by definition. Saggy boobs in my middle age seems a small price to pay for the comfort of my lady lumps in my youth. I glanced down at my chest and realized I probably didn't have a whole lot to worry about, anyway.

"Okay, let's go with that." Darla rolled her eyes. "The point is, I did precisely as I promised. I fixed things. Thanks to my influence and invaluable expertise, you are now dating the hottest and most eligible bachelor in Douglasville. You're welcome."

"I'd like to think maybe I deserve a *little* of the credit." I frowned. "I mean, he seemed interested the night we ran into each other in the ED. You had nothing to do with *that*. And *I* picked out The Dress, not you."

"It *is* a lovely dress, dear." Gran popped a chunk of hot dog in her mouth, gumming it with enthusiasm. "Wasn't it nice of Darla to help you pick it out? Who'd have believed she could be such a sweet girl?"

"Thanks, Gran. Darla didn't pick it out, I did. And since when do you think she's a sweet girl? Weren't you the one who said she was nasty and leopards don't change their spots?"

"When did I say that?" Gran's face wrinkled in thought. "Oh, well. I have early dementia, dear. Can't be held accountable for anything I say. Darla hasn't done anything nasty *lately*. Perhaps death suits her."

"I'll concede to you the *meet-cute* at the ED," Darla allowed, glaring at Gran before returning her attention to me. "*However*, you never would have found The Dress if you didn't go shopping, and I'm the one that convinced you to broaden your horizons. Furthermore, let's not forget it was *my* personal insight that convinced you Jackson isn't simply a Harlan in better packaging. Nor is he—God forbid—a male version of me. Jackson Merritt has character and forms his own opinions, regardless of rumor and innuendo. Admit it, you'd given up on men, convinced you were too freaky to find love. Without my capable guidance, you would have assumed he had ulterior motives, written him off, and never given him a chance."

I considered her claim for a moment. I returned to Douglasville believing I'd risen above the opinion of others, but a few well-placed comments proved to me that despite my personal convictions, I possibly continued to carry a teeny little chip on my shoulder. Without my peculiar, and probably unfair, brand of insider information, I might well have written Jackson off before I'd ever penciled him in. The part of me that would rather French kiss a goat than give Darla the satisfaction of acknowledging her contribution warred with the part that felt compelled to give credit where credit was due.

"I'm sure the dress was simply the icing on the cake, dear," Gran mumbled around a mouthful. "Any fool with eyes in their head can see he's interested, and you have far more to offer than your wardrobe choices. A good thing, considering you sadly lack my fashion flair."

"So, let me see if I've got this straight. Darla takes credit for my capturing Jackson's attention, and you insult the contents of my closet. If I'm not careful, my head will be too big to fit through the door," I muttered, scraping my fork on the plate to capture the last vestiges of cheesy goodness and shoving it into my pie hole.

"Pouting does not become anyone, Lucy, so knock it off," Darla said with a frown. "I'm not taking credit for Jackson's *interest*. I'm simply saying that without my help, you wouldn't have given him a chance to prove he wasn't a shallow, judgmental asshat like the rest of our crowd. And as for your wardrobe." She stared pointedly at my new slippers. "I can't really refute Gran's assessment. However, I would not recommend you follow her fashion example in any way, shape, or form."

"Granted I wasn't initially convinced of Jackson's sincerity. In fact, I'm still not entirely sure I trust any of this. However, I guess I can allow your insight *may* have influenced me somewhat. Although, his turning up to apologize with these awesome slippers said more about him than you ever could. And don't worry, I'm not about to start dressing like Gran. Happy now?"

"Wise decision, dear. Not everyone can carry off my look." Gran rose from the table, gathered the dishes in a small stack, and carried them over to the stove. Setting them on top, she opened the oven, glanced inside, then shook her head with a sigh, and reached for the dishwasher next to it. "Damn, almost got it on the first try that time. Now, if I could find my wallet and my teeth, I'd be cooking with gas."

"Breadbox and cookie jar, respectively," I offered with a smirk. "Darla's been keeping track."

"Well, isn't that nice of her?" Gran retrieved her wallet, stuck it in the waistband of her leggings, and headed for the cookie jar. She felt around inside, held up her dentures triumphantly, and popped them in her mouth. "Going to watch my soaps now. Thank you, Darla, dear."

"No problem, Mrs. A." Darla sighed and looked away as Gran grabbed a chocolate bar from the counter and headed for the living room. I expected she'd be somewhat more pleased with herself, irksomely smug even, since I'd almost confirmed her contribution to my love life.

"Of course, I'm happy, Lucy. You and Jackson are perfect for each other. I knew it all along and feel completely justified in taking partial credit. It's just, well, I said I would stick around until I fixed things, made it up to you for the damage I did in life. And now I guess I have."

"You aren't going to give it up until I say thank you, are you? Okay, fine. Thank you."

"You're welcome." Her smile was sad and fleeting. "I wasn't fishing. I meant if my work here is finished, I guess it's time to move on. I suppose you'll be happy to finally be rid of me."

"Oh." My eyes widened. Sure, not long ago getting rid of Darla was my self-proclaimed mission in life. Now? With the exception of Grandpoppy—who after all, was family—I'd never become attached to a spirit before. Of course, most of them didn't have Darla's tenacity in hanging around long enough to form relationships. I'd grown accustomed to her unwitting condescension and irritating habit of intruding at will. We'd barely tolerated one another in life. Perhaps her death taught us both a few things about one another— and ourselves. I never expected I might actually miss her when she left. I cleared my throat. "So, I guess you've given up on figuring out your cause of death?"

"No, I didn't give up. I simply remembered." Darla shook her head and glided back to the top of the fridge to set up the cereal boxes when Mr. Picklepaw, abandoned by Gran in favor of her afternoon addiction, hopped up and whacked them over. "Bee sting."

"Huh?"

"You remember I told you I went into the restroom and cracked the window because of the heat? Not the best move in retrospect. The stinging I felt behind my ear was a yellow jacket who apparently saw the open window as an invitation. So anticlimactic, don't you think? All those nefarious possibilities right down the crapper. It wasn't the Botox. It was the bee. I'd never been stung before. It appears I'm terribly allergic. Who knew?" She shrugged. "I mean, if I ever suspected, I would have carried one of those handy dandy little emergency pen thingies."

"In a jewel encrusted designer case, no doubt."

"Naturally." The corners of Darla's lips tilted up. "Monogrammed."

"The autopsy indicated anaphylaxis and massive inflammation. The Botox seemed the obvious culprit," I offered lamely. I mean, what could I say? Whether Botox or bee sting, the end result was the same. Darla died.

"Of course. And realistically, it's just the trigger that changed. I'm dead in any case. Still, it's a relief to know the truth."

"I guess. I'm sorry, Darla."

"Thanks. Me, too. You know, Lucy, if I'd been a less shallow, self-absorbed bitch in life, I like to think I would have seen you as someone worth getting to know. Maybe we could have been friends."

"Well, thank you. Maybe if you'd been a less shallow, self-absorbed bitch in life, I would have seen you as someone worth getting to know, too." I drew in a deep breath. "We got something few people ever get, didn't we? A second chance. Maybe the prospect of eternity in an ugly, purple velour track suit humbles a girl, but you aren't nearly the snob you used to be. And I think…I think maybe now we understand one another better on a lot of levels. Maybe we *are* friends, Darla. In a supernatural, dysfunctional way, of course," I qualified quickly in case she didn't feel the same way.

"I'm inclined to agree, however, a *real* friend would not remind me of my gawd-awful attire. Among my many regrets, choosing this monstrosity of an outfit to die in will always rank in the top three. I mean, seriously, what was I thinking?"

"Don't ask me. You and Gran already determined I'm fashion challenged, remember?"

"I'm kidding. I know exactly what I was thinking. I figured no one would give me a second glance in this atrocious eyesore of an ensemble, and my little visit to the clinic would go undetected. A tragic miscalculation on my part. As for you, you've been wallowing in poor fashion choices for far too long. Scrubs are simple. Jeans with tees are easy. They're comfortable and familiar. When it comes to clothes, you follow the path of least resistance. Take chances, Lucy. You have taste, you just need to trust it."

"I'm not you, Darla. Comfortable and familiar works for me."

"For the love of hot fudge! Then promise me you'll at least accessorize occasionally," she cried, throwing her hands in the air. "Honestly, Lucy Ashcroft, how do you expect a girl to move on and rest in peace when there is every possibility the best friend she ever had runs the risk of being mistaken for a bag lady?"

The best friend she ever had? I barely had time to process the warm, fuzzy feeling her words evoked and formulate a reply before the doorbell chimed and Darla disappeared. She returned before I'd reached the hall, concern creasing her features, her ghostly complexion a shade paler.

"Quick, call the police and send Gran upstairs to lock herself in her room. It's Harlan, and he's drunk as a skunk. It's never his finest hour. Harlan is as mean as a hill of fire ants when he's sozzled, and he's gunning for you."

Chapter Seventeen

Harlan soon abandoned the superficial politeness of the bell, opting instead to hammer on the door with his fists. Working in an Emergency Department, I had extensive experience with surly, intoxicated people. However, they generally didn't direct their ire at me, personally. My heart pounded in rhythm to Harlan's incessant thumping, nearly drowning out Gran's loud protests about missing the end of her show and being deprived of ever learning the identity of the illegitimate triplet's biological father. Having done time as a soap opera addict, I reassured her she could tune in six months from now and pick up precisely where she left off. I scooped up Mr. Picklepaw, who'd followed me into the hall, and shoved him at my grandmother, while hustling them both up the stairs.

Once I knew Gran was safely ensconced in her boudoir with her furry friend, I verified the chain lock was intact on the front door, blew out a shaky breath, and turned the knob. Harlan Hampton IV apparently perceived the two-inch gap as an open invitation. His pounding ceased, and his ranting commenced.

The alcohol fumes seeping through the crack were strong enough to singe my eyebrows, and he'd imbibed enough to preclude most intelligible speech. However, he managed to pronounce the term conniving bitch with surprising clarity. Darla flitted nervously back and forth through the door, and a sudden chill in the vicinity of my ankles alerted me to the fact Chloe had arrived and taken up a position in front of me. She couldn't actually protect me—at least I didn't think she could—but, she didn't know that. It warmed the cockles of my heart that Jackson's dog liked me enough to try. Even if she was dead.

"Harlan, you are shit-faced, stinking drunk," I stated when he paused for breath at last. "Go home and sleep it off."

"You knew, *Looschy*," he slurred. "You tricked me. Give me the cat."

"I didn't trick you, Harlan. You didn't want the cat," I returned evenly. I've discovered when dealing with children and drunks, it's best to maintain a calm, reasonable tone and use small words. "You aren't a cat person, remember?"

"I am when the little bastard is my meal ticket." Harlan rattled the knob and shoved against the door, sounding less intoxicated and more threatening by the second. "Hand him over."

"What are you waiting for?" Darla wrung her hands, as the door shuddered again. "Call the police!"

"I—" Chloe leaped through the door snarling, as Harlan slammed his weight against it for the third time, and the brackets securing the chain gave way.

"Too late," Darla announced unnecessarily. I jumped back as the door flew open and banged off the wall. "Hurry, turn on every light you can...oh, and the TV, too."

"Why?" I gasped, backing away from the angry figure advancing on me, fists clenched at his sides, flicking switches as I went.

"Just do it!" Darla screeched, perching on top of the television. "And pray this works."

"No one makes a fool of me," Harlan growled, plodding unsteadily in my direction. "Especially not Lucy the Ghost Gabber."

"No one needs to, Harlan. You do a bang up job of it all by your lonesome." I reached behind me, feeling for the remote. I snatched it from the coffee table and aimed it at the boob tube. The box sprang to life, and Darla disappeared inside. If she'd hoped Gran's soap opera would distract Harlan, her plan failed. He clearly had zero interest in the identity of the illegitimate triplet's biological father. I scurried around the sofa, trying to put any kind of barrier between Harlan and me, as cheesy organ music cued the end of the show. The lights flickered, the television crackled and buzzed. As Harlan lunged, the screen went black and exploded, along with all the lightbulbs in the room, sending shards of glass everywhere.

"Was that really necessary?" I muttered, before Harlan's strangled gasp revealed exactly why Darla trashed my living room. She reappeared in the center of the room, and her bereaved husband's frozen stance, bulging eyes, and sickly pallor alerted me to the fact I wasn't the only one who saw her. Well, I'd been contemplating the purchase of a new flat screen, and at least she spared my laptop battery this time.

"Harlan Henry Hampton, you swaggering son of a sniveling sea monkey," Darla shrieked, zipping across the room until she hovered nose to nose with her stunned spouse. "Who do you think you are showing up here snockered and threatening my friend?"

Harlan's mouth fell open. He squeezed his eyes

shut and shook his head. Taking a deep breath, he blew it out and cracked a tentative lid. Groping for the nearest chair, he dropped into it, eyes wide and fixed on his purple velour clad wife. "Cripes, I must've drank more than I thought. I still see her. It's not possible."

"Oh, I'm relatively sure it is." I smirked. "Welcome to my world, Harlan."

"You mean she's real?"

"Of course, I'm real, you dimwit," Darla huffed, crossing her arms over her no longer transparent chest. "If I was a figment of your imagination, I'd be better dressed, don't you think?"

"What in the hell are you wearing, anyway?" Harlan sputtered. "That isn't what you were buried in. I may have let you down more often than not in life, but I made damn sure you went out in style."

"Though I appreciate the effort, what I *actually* went out in was purple velour," Darla sighed. "May I suggest you ditch your lucky golf pants? Trust me, darling, if lightning strikes on the eighteenth hole, you do *not* want to spend eternity in orange and green plaid polyester."

"I can't believe this. The keys that kept going missing, the car radio turning itself on, the flickering lights, the rattling doorknobs—all those things I chalked up to guilt or my imagination—it was you." Harlan stared a moment longer, then sat forward and dropped his head into his hands.

"And the bourbon, Harlan. Don't underestimate the hallucinogenic properties of habitual daily overindulgence in a fine Kentucky blend." Darla snorted.

"Yeah. Well, it helps keep me from looking too

closely at myself." He raised his head, and some of the color returned to his face. "It was you all along, wasn't it? You're haunting me."

"Technically she's haunting me," I pointed out. "I'll share. I'm a giver."

"I suppose I can't blame you," he continued as though I hadn't spoken. "I made your life miserable, and then I traded the deposit on my liposuction and got you the Botox certificate instead, and it killed you."

"You planned on having liposuction?" Darla raised a brow.

"Chelsea, this uh, woman I met online, worked for the doctor." He had the courtesy to flush. "Got me a deep discount. Sounded like a simple way to get my body back in shape while avoiding all the diet and exercise. You know how I hate diet and exercise. I thought it was a great idea until I had the consult and understood the post procedure discomfort involved. I don't do pain, Darla."

"Unless you're inflicting it, apparently. You know what, Harlan? You did make my life miserable." Darla looked away, blinking rapidly. "I was the richest, prettiest, most popular girl in Douglasville. I took care of myself. I kept a beautiful home. I gave the most elegant parties. And I loved you. Why wasn't it good enough? Why wasn't *I* good enough?"

"It wasn't you. It was me." Harlan held up a hand when I opened my mouth.

"Oh-Em-Gee! You did *not* just try that tired old line," Darla huffed.

"I know, I know. Cliché, right? Doesn't mean it isn't true. Star jock, money to burn, and the most beautiful, desirable girl in town wearing my ring. I had it all, right? A real big shot. Then, I woke up one morning and realized we weren't in high school anymore. I had no marketable skills, no head for business, and all those things I thought made me important were transient. I was a fraud. And I knew some morning you'd wake up and realize it, too."

"So, armed with this newfound insight, you decided to facilitate my epiphany by gambling us into a hole deeper than the Grand Canyon, drinking like a sailor with a wooden leg, and boinking anything in a skirt?" Darla's brows slammed together. "Your consideration touches me more than I can say."

"Maybe I'll run upstairs and check on Gran." I sidestepped toward the hall, thinking I should give them a little privacy. Harlan's drunken rage had abated. Funny how sobering an appearance by the ghost of your dead wife can be.

"No!" Cried Harlan and Darla in unison wearing identical looks of concern.

"I'm fading." She held out her hands, which did look more transparent than they had a moment ago. "Of course, given the age of that television of yours, and Gran's love of fifteen watt bulbs, I'm surprised I had enough juice to materialize in the first place. You really need to move into the modern era, Lucy. High definition flat screens and LEDs. Anyway, I need you. I'm determined to finish this conversation now that we're finally having it. If Harlan can't see me, he can't hear me, either. You'll have to interpret."

Swell. Just what I aspired to when I woke up this morning—marriage counselor to the drunk and dead. I rolled my eyes so hard my head hurt, pushed out my bottom lip, and schlepped across the room to the sofa.

"Fine." I planted my ass and waved a hand in the air. "Let's wrap it up before I decide to start speaking my mind. Not that I have a problem speaking my mind. Nonetheless, doing it with any degree of tact at the moment could prove challenging."

"I understand completely." Darla nodded. Planting her fists on her hips, she spun back to face Harlan, and arched a brow. "Well?"

"I thought sleeping with other women would validate I was still important, still big man on campus. It didn't. It only proved I had less to recommend me than I gave myself credit for." He scrubbed his hands over his face and dropped his chin to his chest. "I never intended to hurt you, Darla."

"Well, you did hurt me," she whispered in a choked voice, wringing her hands together. She faded to nearly full transparency.

"I know, and then I killed you. You deserved so much better than you got from me. I did love you, Darla. I'd trade places with you if I could." Harlan raised red-rimmed eyes, then shot to his feet, glancing around wildly. "Where did she go?"

"She's still here," I said quietly. "You just can't see her anymore."

"I wanted to tell her I'm sorry," He moaned on a shaky breath. His shoulders shook. "I'm so sorry."

Darla gasped and pressed her fingers to her lips. "I think he truly means it." Her chin quivered, but her eyes shone. "And he loved me, Lucy."

"Of course, he did." I rose to my feet and stepped forward intending to lay a comforting hand on Harlan's arm. Then I changed my mind. Though he'd managed to make Darla feel better, I still thought of him as a bilious sack of goat slime. He really didn't deserve comforting in my book. Sue me. "It's okay, Harlan. She heard you fine."

I doubted I would ever cultivate any real fondness for Harlan Hampton IV. However, the fact his obvious grief and genuine regret gave Darla comfort induced me to loathe the asshat just a tiny bit less. For now. I couldn't guarantee my softened attitude would continue if he demanded the return of Mr. Picklepaw again.

"And you didn't kill her, Harlan. A yellow jacket did. Not even Darla knew she was allergic."

"You're only saying that to make me feel better," Harlan muttered.

"Actually, I don't like you well enough to want to make you feel better. The sting is behind her left ear. I suppose you could request an exhumation and a new autopsy. Or you could simply believe I have insider information and let it go."

"Thank you." He cleared his throat and tried to reach for my hand, which I artfully shoved in my pocket. "You've been remarkably decent considering I broke down your front door."

"You know, Harlan, Tillie left that money in trust, with specific directions. It's not as though you could have gotten your hands on it for personal use, even if you had possession of the cat. So, how about you leave my grandmother and the cat alone—and pay to replace the chain—and we'll forget it ever happened. Deal?"

"Deal. And for the record, I never actually believed it when Darla said you saw dead people."

"Neither did Darla. Imagine *her* surprise." Darla responded by thumbing her nose at me.

"I guess I should be going." Harlan shuffled his

feet, twisting his fingers together. "So, uh, thanks."

"For what?"

"For helping me tell Darla the things I needed to say."

"That had nothing to do with me, Harlan. You could have said those things anytime. She's been hanging around. She'd have heard you." Personally, I thought Darla probably needed to hear those things a lot more than Harlan needed to say them.

"Maybe, but without you, I wouldn't know that. Oh, and I guess I should thank you for not calling the cops and pressing charges, too." Color flooded his face.

"Yeah, you probably should." I bit back a grin.

"So, I guess I'll leave now." He took a step back.

"Okie dokie. Don't let the door hit you in the ass."

He nodded stiffly and turned to go.

"Lucy," Darla hissed in my ear. "Tell him I forgive him."

"What?" I asked. Harlan paused. Damn, I'd been so close to getting rid of him.

"Tell him," she insisted.

"Um, Harlan?" I cleared my throat. He turned to face me. "Darla said she forgives you."

His mouth opened and closed several times like a dying fish. Then, to my utter horror, he reached out and yanked me into a bear hug, mashing my face into his sweat dampened and booze stained shirt. Um, ew? Someone coughed as I struggled to free myself from the unwelcome—and unsanitary—embrace. I finally thrust my arms against him, hard and gained relative freedom. A man stood directly behind Harlan Hampton IV, a bottle of wine in one hand and a bag of groceries in the other. His dark brows disappeared into his hairline, and he dropped the bag and bottle on the chair before crossing his arms over his chest. His wide, magnificent chest. Chloe trotted in from the front porch and planted herself at his feet as he looked from me to Harlan, and back to me again.

"Someone care to explain what's going on?

Chapter Eighteen

Harlan took that as his cue and beat a hasty retreat without another word. After announcing Gran's dentures were in the mailbox, Darla, the traitorous witch, streamed out right behind him. His heavy footsteps pounded across the porch and down the stairs as I struggled to untie my tongue.

"Jackson. What are you doing here?" I sputtered at last.

"After thinking about you all morning, I realized I didn't want to wait until Saturday night to see you again. I thought—hoped—maybe you felt the same way. So, I figured I'd pick up a couple of things and come over and cook dinner for you and your grandmother. Elderly women cannot survive on Chinese take-out and peanut butter alone. Clearly, you found other things to keep yourself occupied until the weekend."

"I know you aren't implying what I think you're implying." Crossing my arms over *my* chest, I raised *my* brows and dared him to accuse me of having a little *sumpin-sumpin* going on with Harlan Hampton IV. Honestly, I didn't know if I could remain halfway in love with a man who gave me so little credit. Although I would certainly continue to date him. I mean, I'm not a total moron. "I'd rather lick the floor of the gas station bathroom, get a pap smear, swap spit with a camel—"

"I meant fending off slobbering drunks. I could smell him from the porch. What did *you* think I meant?" He smiled and opened his arms. I stepped right into them and laid my cheek against his chest. Needless to say, it was a vast improvement over Harlan's. "Are you okay? Do I need to kick his flabby ass?"

"Wearing pointy boots?"

"Will it earn me extra points?" Laughter rumbled beneath my ear.

"Absolutely." I smiled into his shirtfront.

"In that case, I think it can be arranged." He pulled back to look down into my face. "Seriously, Lucy. Did he give you a hard time?"

"He started to, but then Darla made an appearance. I think she shocked him sober," I replied with a smile.

"When you say she made an appearance—"

"Behold." I released his waist with one hand and swept my arm across the room. His eyes widened, and a long, low whistle escaped his lips as he took stock of the broken glass littering the floor. And the gaping hole in the television screen. "Our little Darla has mastered the fine art of materializing."

"I'm so proud." Jackson shook his head and raised his voice. "Maybe next she can learn to clean up after herself?"

"Save your breath." I laughed. "She's not here. She took off hot on Harlan's heels."

"Typical Darla. Make a mess and leave it for someone else to worry about." He set me away from him. "You grab the dustpan, and I'll get dinner started. Gran can play sous chef until you're free. Where is she, by the way?"

"Peanut butter fudge! I sent her and Mr. Picklepaw

to her room when Harlan showed up." I slipped from Jackson's embrace and hurried to the foot of the stairs. "Gran, you can come down now."

"Sure, now that I missed the end of my show," Gran grumbled as her bedroom door creaked open. Mr. Picklepaw streaked by in a blur heading for his litterbox. "Maybe you could whip up a batch of those instant mashed potatoes? They'll go nicely with the leftover Chinese. A person could starve up there waiting for you to call the all clear. Oh well. At least it gave me an excuse to spend some quality time with BOB."

"Gran, Jackson's here," I hissed as my face went up in flames. Again, I say there are simply some things about your grandmother you do *not* want to know.

"Who's Bob?" Jackson asked, hefting the bag in his arms. You also do not want to explain them to your hot new boyfriend.

"You will never be able to unsee the automatic visual which accompanies the knowledge. Trust me." I stepped aside as Gran reached the bottom. Desperate to change the subject before she decided to elaborate, I pointed to the exceedingly attractive man with the wine and food in his arms. "Jackson's going to cook dinner for us."

"So, no instant spuds?" Gran asked.

"Steak, oven roasted potatoes, and asparagus," Jackson announced with a wink in my direction. "I hope that's okay?"

"Steak?" Gran shot me a worried glance.

"Mailbox," I offered.

"That's a new one." Gran shuffled out to the porch. There was a screech of metal, and then she reappeared in the doorway with full dentition and a wide grin. "Steak, huh? Well, that's all right then."

"Come on, Mrs. Ashcroft." Jackson chuckled, striding toward the kitchen. "While Lucy sweeps up Darla's mess, and I season the meat, you can scrub the potatoes."

"Call me Beulah, dear. Or better yet, Gran." Gran shoved up her sleeves and turned on the faucet, as Jackson deposited his haul on the counter and passed her a bag of tiny potatoes. I retrieved the dustpan from behind the laundry room door, and started back toward the living room. Gran's next words stopped me in my tracks. "I mean, now you're dancing the Recumbent Rhumba with my granddaughter, Mrs. Ashcroft does seem a bit formal."

"Oh, we're not...I mean, we haven't..." Jackson stuttered, a faint flush creeping up from the neck of his black T-shirt.

"Oh, you will," Gran announced in a cheerful voice. I ducked my head to conceal my flaming cheeks, yanked open the nearest drawer, and felt around blindly until I snagged a vegetable brush. I shoved it into her hand and leaned close.

"Filters, Gran. Filters," I murmured in her ear.

"Filters, my arse!" Gran slammed the utensil on the counter and spun to face the two of us, fists planted on her spandex clad hips. "I may be an old woman who pees when I sneeze, can't keep track of my teeth, and sometimes forgets what day it is. I'll also admit to an unhealthy attachment to leather garments of any kind, but that's not relevant to the current discussion. The point is, one thing I am *not*, is blind. Life is short, children. When kindred souls collide, when a chance at happiness slaps you upside the head, you don't pussyfoot around stammering and blushing, you grab it. Have I made myself clear?" She arched a bushy brow, fixing a glare on first one of us, and then the other.

"So, you're suggesting we—?" Jackson choked, fighting the upward curl of his lips, and capturing my gaze with a meaningful stare.

"Suggesting is for sissies. I'm telling you straight up. Throw caution to the wind. Embrace your destiny. Get jiggy with it, dear." Gran nodded curtly and reached into the lower cabinet for a baking dish. She dumped the freshly scrubbed, and neatly halved, baby spuds into the pan, and proceeded to drizzle olive oil and apply the appropriate mix of seasoning with no direction whatsoever. "Not right this minute, of course. I'm starving and this is the first chance for a decent, home-cooked meal I've had since Lucy moved in and decided the kitchen was off-limits to me."

"You broiled the African violets," I pointed out.

"One little oversight and suddenly everyone's a critic," she grumbled, shoving the vegetables in the oven and slamming the door. I watched in amazement as she took a pot from the overhead rack, filled it with water and a liberal pinch of salt, and set it on the stove to boil. She reached around Jackson, grabbed the bunch of asparagus, and removed the plastic wrap from the thick, green stalks, again without hesitation, or a single cue. "It was your fault for setting them next to the artichokes. Don't you have something to clean? Like the poor, shattered remains of my television, and the last of my collection of fifteen watt bulbs? Damn that Darla Swithers."

"I'll buy you a new television, Gran." I laughed,

grinning at Jackson. He smiled back, his eyes alight with something I hardly dared hope for. Surely he realized by now both Gran and I were a little left of center, but every word, every glance, every action, made it increasingly clear he didn't have a problem veering from the straight and narrow. Could I trust it? A grandmother I adored, the man I'd always dreamed of, and the promise of a steak dinner. What more could a girl ask?

"Sixty-inch flat screen with high definition?" Gran's expression brightened.

"Sure, why not?" I laughed, heading for the living room.

"Surround sound would be lovely," she persisted as I reached the hall.

"Why on earth do you need surround sound?" I turned in exasperation.

"Maybe she enjoys movie night." Jackson caught my eye and winked, before turning his attention to trimming the meat. Chloe sprawled at his feet, tongue lolling. No doubt she hoped a stray beef trimming might accidentally fall to the floor. Not that she could eat it, but the poor pup apparently hadn't figured it out yet.

"While I'm sure I'd enjoy a total theater experience in the comfort of my own home as much as the next old biddy, what really snaps my elastic is The Hair Band Channel, dear." She waggled her brows and smacked her lips. "Dancercise is my fitness regimen of choice, and that Jon Bon Jovi has got one hell of a set of pipes."

"I thought we agreed there would be no more twerking?" I sighed, closing my eyes to blot out the memory of our last trip to the neurologist when Gran demonstrated reflexes the doctor never dreamed of testing. To borrow a phrase from Darla, Oh-Em-Gee.

"We agreed there would be no more twerking *in public*," Gran conceded, perm-curled locks bobbing along with her head. "However, this is my house. What happens in the living room, stays in the living room."

"Seems reasonable," Jackson observed, flipping the steaks on the broiler pan to season the other side. I stood in the kitchen doorway, gripping the dustpan, and mesmerized by the sight of him. The lock of dark hair tumbling over his forehead, the comfortable self-assurance of his stance, and the flexing of bunched muscles beneath the tight cotton as he worked. His long, skilled fingers gently poked and prodded the meat, massaging the herbs into the flesh, and I squeezed my thighs together and swallowed a groan as I pictured them stroking and kneading something altogether different.

As though reading my mind, Jackson paused in his task and shot me a smoldering look over his shoulder. Locking my knees to avoid face-planting right there on the linoleum floor, I cleared my throat and tossed my head with an exaggerated degree of nonchalance.

"It's settled then," I croaked. "Surround sound it is."

Gran clapped her hands, then picked up the asparagus and plunked it in the boiling water. She followed it up by rummaging around in the silverware drawer until she came up with a corkscrew and proceeded to open the wine. I shook my head, wondering where this Gourmet Network star had been hiding for the past six months. Wielding my trusty dustpan, I traipsed to the living room to sweep up the glass.

Thirty minutes and forty trillion, two hundred and eighty-five million, nine hundred and fifty-seven pieces of glass later—apparently a couple of lightbulbs and an ancient television screen under the influence of an agitated spirit can shatter into enough particles to pave Main Street—Jackson called out dinner was ready. I hauled myself to my feet and followed the enticing aroma of broiling beef into the kitchen. The table was set, the wine poured, and Gran's butt was parked at the table, potatoes stacked on her plate, and ladling—oh, sweet mother—béarnaise sauce over her asparagus. I dumped the glass shards into the trash and hurried to the sink to wash the dust—and blood—from my fingers. I slid into a chair as Jackson piled the sizzling meat onto a platter and carried it to the table.

"Dig in," he urged with a smile. "I bragged, so now I'm a guy with something to prove."

And prove it, he did. The entire meal could have tasted like sawdust, and I doubt I would have complained—or noticed. The absolute perfection of the juicy steaks, the crispy, browned potatoes, the tender asparagus with creamy, golden béarnaise, and the ruby radiance of the Chianti took my breath away. But, what really tightened my chest and made it difficult to breathe was the gleam in Jackson's dark eyes regarding me steadily throughout the meal over the glow of the flickering candle. I decided it must have been Gran's idea—it was citronella—but it did add a certain ambiance.

Gran, meanwhile, worked those dentures with the efficiency and determination of a wood chipper, had seconds of everything, and gulped her wine with an alacrity that alarmed me. Finally, she set down her knife and fork, and pushed her plate away.

"Not since my Eugene have I met a man so easy on the eye who can cook, too." Gran relaxed in her chair with a sigh and fixed her gaze on me. "Lucy, I've decided we're keeping him."

Chapter Nineteen

Though it took some convincing, I finally persuaded Jackson to escort Gran to the back porch for a post dinner glass of wine while I cleaned up. My talent for loading the dishwasher rivaled my culinary skills, but since he'd prepared the feast, it seemed only fair. Which didn't mean I wanted an audience.

"Don't discount your grandmother's opinion. Beulah always did have impeccable taste in men," Grandpoppy observed as I loaded the dishwasher. "Obviously."

"I'm not discounting her opinion. I'm simply pointing out that Jackson is not Mr. Picklepaw. We can't just decide to *keep* him. And you shouldn't eavesdrop." I slammed the dishwasher, dried my hands, and combed my fingers through my hair. I frowned at my palms, realizing what I'd done. Then I scrubbed and dried my hands again. Nurses have a bit of a fetish about handwashing.

"I don't eavesdrop, pumpkin. I've been parked on top of the fridge for the last forty minutes. You were too preoccupied by that juicy piece of meat to notice."

"Jackson is not a juicy piece of meat," I huffed.

"How disappointing." Jackson interjected in a voice as dry as the Chianti. He stepped through the screen door, wine glasses in hand and the empty bottle tucked under one arm. Gran wobbled along beside him

171

clinging to the other. "All those hours sweating in the gym wasted. I take it Darla's back?"

"No, actually it's my grandfather." I narrowed my eyes in Grandpoppy's direction. "And he's being crass."

"Hello, Eugene, dear," Gran shouted. "Are you staying?"

"What's crass about admiring a nice cut of beef? Always did enjoy a good steak," Grandpoppy guffawed. "Not my fault your mind's splashing around in the gutter. Good evening, Beulah, my sweet. And yes, I'm staying."

"Grandpoppy says hello, Gran." I sighed. "And he's here for the night."

"That's all right, then. Oh, I am *so* tired." Her free hand fluttered in front of her mouth as she indulged in an exaggerated, and completely bogus, yawn. She patted Jackson's arm and released it. "Think I'll head upstairs. It's way past my bed time."

"It's six forty-five." I pressed my lips together to keep from laughing at her obvious ploy.

"Exhaustion doesn't wear a wristwatch, dear. I suppose it's the wine," Gran ventured. "I think it's best if I sleep it off."

"You had one glass," I pointed out.

"It's probably interacting with my blood pressure pills," she suggested.

"You don't take blood pressure pills."

"Heart medication?" Her expression was hopeful.

"Nope."

"Baby aspirin?" Her face fell when I shook my head at her last ditch effort.

"Nice try." I grinned. With the exception of an

occasional acetaminophen for aches and pains, Gran took no regularly scheduled medication. Quite a remarkable accomplishment for an eighty-five-year-old. Of course, Gran was quite a remarkable woman. At least, I thought so. "For your information, you are the worst actress I've ever seen."

"For your information, the Soap Opera Marathon Channel reruns The Haves and Have Nots every night at seven o'clock. Sue me for attempting a polite exit. Thank you, Jackson, dear. I enjoyed dinner immensely. However, I refuse to allow Darla Swithers' attention grabbing stunt to deprive me of the opportunity to confirm my theory. The father is Raoul," Gran announced confidently, narrowing her eyes at me. "You've got a television in your room. Though it only has a twenty-five inch screen, I am willing to make the sacrifice and slum it, just this once. Therefore, consider yourself on notice I am commandeering your room for the night."

"I see." I glanced at Jackson. His dark eyes twinkled and his lips twitched. "My alarm clock is in there you know. How am I supposed to get up for work? You know mornings are not my friend."

"You don't have work tomorrow." Gran crossed her arms over her ample, if saggy, bosoms. "And even if you did, you do have a cell phone, don't you?"

"Yeah, so?"

"Get with the program, dear. There's an app for that." Gran rolled her eyes so hard she listed to the side. Jackson reached out to steady her, and she slapped his hand away. "I'm fine."

"Of course, you are. I just wanted to give you a kiss good-night, and thank you for acting as sous chef."

Jackson bent and pressed his lips to Gran's tissue paper cheek. "I couldn't have done it without you."

"That's bull hockey, and you know it." Gran waved him away, a becoming rose staining her cheeks. "Still, it's extremely gallant of you to say so. Isn't he gallant, Lucy?"

"He is, indeed, Gran." He was also stunningly attractive, built like a Michelangelo sculpture, and a culinary genius. But his patience and humor, along with his kindness—especially toward my grandmother—gained him another piece of my heart. I never believed in love at first sight. In fact, given my unique situation, I doubted I'd ever find love, at all. And Jackson didn't believe in ghosts. In a very short time, we'd both seen our beliefs challenged and kicked to the curb. I was falling in love with Jackson Merritt. Unexpected? Duh. Unlikely? Hell, yeah. Unwise? Probably. But, the look in his eyes when I gazed at him with no attempt to conceal my feelings, allowed the hope I'd long ago abandoned to rise to the surface.

Gran's head swiveled from me to Jackson and back again, a speculative gleam in her eyes. "I guess I'll be off, then," she announced, and tottered into the hall.

"G'night, Gran. Love you."

"Love you, too, Lucy." She paused at the bottom of the stairs. "By the way, if you wanted to, oh, I don't know, head over to Jackson's to see his etchings? I'll be fine. Eugene will be here."

"Duly noted." I laughed. Gran's dearth of acting talent was eclipsed only by her absolute absence of subtlety.

Once the bedroom door banged shut overhead, Jackson's arms slipped around me from behind, his hot breath ruffling my hair as he feathered his lips along the side of my neck. My lady parts sang. I sagged against him, striving to remain vertical with bones the consistency of butter.

"So, about those etchings," Jackson whispered in my ear before nipping at the lobe.

"Do you actually *have* etchings?" I squirmed in his arms, feeling the hard length of him straining against the front of his jeans and pressing against my backside.

"Um, no. However, I *do* have a collection of antique embalming tools that's kind of fascinating," he said, sweeping my hair aside with his hand. Then he proceeded to nibble his way up the nape of my neck.

"You certainly know how to tempt a girl, Mr. Merritt." I snorted, turning in his arms and locking my hands behind his neck. "I bet once you let *that* cat out of the bag, you have to beat women off with a stick."

Jackson chuckled, before his expression turned deadly serious. He cupped my jaw, burying his fingers in the hair on either side of my head, and lowered his face to mine. His hand slid around to the nape of my neck, and he deepened the kiss. His tongue traced the seam of my lips and swept inside, seeking, stroking, plundering with the ferocity of a man dying of thirst who'd discovered my lips were an endless spring. When he raised his head at last, my breathing was as harsh and ragged as his. He touched his forehead to mine, then released me and spun away. Fists clenched at his sides, he stared out the back door into the rapidly darkening twilight.

"What is it?" I gasped, the confusion in my voice evident to my own ears.

"I need a minute." His sigh sounded more like a

frustrated growl vibrating in his chest.

"You need a minute?" I echoed like a mindless parrot, a feeling of unease churning in my gut.

"Look, it's not you, it's me," he responded.

The words echoed in my head like a death knell. Everyone knows any discourse beginning with that lead-in had nowhere to go except downhill. I shivered as his words hit me like a bucket of ice water, bringing me back to reality. He was wrong. It *was* me. The freaky girl who sees dead people is the one who misread patience, humor, and kindness, together with an apparent acceptance of my gift, and a little heated flirtation, as the promise of something more. I wrapped it all up in a romantic fantasy package of happily ever after, slapped a bow on it, and called it Christmas. While he didn't exactly discourage me, I knew better. If it had been anyone other than Jackson Merritt, I wouldn't have lowered my guard so quickly, so readily, or so completely. My heart plummeted, landing with a sad, wet plop on the kitchen floor.

"I see." I cleared my throat, but the tightness persisted. Impending tears have that effect on me. "Listen, Jackson. I get it. Dinner was great. Gran enjoyed it so much. Maybe I should learn to cook, huh? Anyway, thanks. For everything. It's been fun."

"It's been *fun*?" Jackson turned slowly, his brows drawn together over a thunderous expression. "I've thought about you nearly every minute of every day since you crashed into me outside the ER. I've lain awake at night thinking up excuses to spend more time with you that wouldn't seem calculated and contrived. I referred a long time client to another funeral director to avoid interfering with our dinner plans for Saturday.

I'm a man who doesn't do impetuous, yet purchased elephant slippers—*elephant slippers*—on a whim. You are completely unlike any woman I've ever known, or hoped to find. There's enough chemistry between us to detonate an atom bomb, and I'm ready to explode with wanting you. And we both know you wouldn't have said no."

"You're right. I wouldn't have said no," I whispered through stiff lips. "How fortunate you're quite capable of saying it for both of us."

"This whole thing is so far outside my comfort zone I might need a map to find my way back. I'm tied in knots wrestling with the absolute lunacy of feeling this much this quickly, and meanwhile, you're having *fun*. Well, I'm glad you found me an entertaining diversion, Lucy. I guess I was the fool thinking it was something more."

Before I could pick up my jaw from the floor to respond, he opened the back door and disappeared into the darkness. He thought it was something more? I lifted a foot to follow, to call him back, to explain, but a stabbing pain in my head sent me to my knees. I lay sprawled on the cold linoleum, eyes squeezed shut, grinding my molars together, and wondering what a ruptured aneurysm felt like. I would die here, alone, on a kitchen floor the seventies had been trying to reclaim for forty years. Gran would be left all alone with a tri-testicular cat, a twenty-five inch television, and no macaroni and cheese with franks. Tears of regret trickled from the corners of my eyes and ran into my ears. Jackson would never know *I* thought it was something more, too.

"For the love of Rocky Road, must you be such a

drama queen? It was just a little slap in the head."

My eyes snapped open to find Darla hovering above me, arms akimbo and eyes rolling. It wasn't an aneurysm. I wasn't dying. The bitch had given me brain freeze.

"Do you have any idea how much that hurts?" I grumbled, climbing slowly to my feet. "I would totally kill you if you weren't already dead."

"Do you have any idea how little I care?" She snapped back. "After all I've done. How could you stand there with your tongue hanging out like a winded dog and let him walk away? What were you thinking?"

"I was thinking I'd stop him, before someone, who in actuality has done far less than she gives herself credit for, inserted her surgically enhanced snout where it didn't belong, yet again." I glared. Which at the moment probably hurt me far worse than it hurt Darla.

"Oh." She blinked. "Well, in my defense, I had no idea a little love tap would have such an effect. May I offer my deepest regrets? Now, get your ass in gear, and go after him."

"That could be a little difficult considering I have no idea where he went," I sighed.

"Minor detail. I do. Or rather, I will." She disappeared, returning in the blink of an eye. "He's headed for the Country Club."

"Well, that takes care of that. It's members only, or had you forgotten? My membership seems to have lapsed. My bad."

"Money might buy a cute little card. It doesn't buy class, Lucy. You're as good as anyone there, and don't you forget it, no matter what anyone says."

"Including you?" I smirked.

"Especially me. Sometimes my words have a tendency to exit my lips before my brain decides if it's a good idea. Now, stop sulking, get changed, and run a comb through the rat's nest currently masquerading as your hair. It also wouldn't hurt to put on a little mascara." She fired orders at me like a drill sergeant, ticking off each directive on her fingers.

"Pay attention Darla, *Members Only*. A little black dress and all the class in the world won't get me through the door."

"No, but I know exactly what will." She grinned. "Trust me. You won't be sorry."

Chapter Twenty

Darla's ingenious plan consisted of driving to her former home, banging on her former door, and demanding Harlan Hampton IV fork over his guest pass for the Country Club. To give her credit, it worked beautifully. Especially once I helped him overcome his initial reluctance by threatening to disclose the extent of his infidelities to his grieving in-laws. Darla's parents—coincidentally—were currently paying Harlan's mortgage and helping keep the wolves from his door, thanks to a sadly misplaced sense of responsibility. Thus motivated, Harlan slapped the laminated little *carte blanche* in my hand, *tout suite*. He even managed to do so with a pasted on smile—although it could have been a grimace.

While Darla went on ahead, I drove the short distance to the Country Club, replaying the scene with Jackson over and over in my mind. By the time I pulled up under the scalloped awning, climbed out of my car, and handed my keys to the valet, my mood progressed from upset to downright incensed. I stalked up the stairs, flashed my pass at the doorman, and strode between the white, marble pillars and into the vestibule like I owned the place. The hushed, elegant atmosphere reeked of entitlement and old money. I sensed none of the bad juju Gran had transiently alluded to when I mentioned our dinner date. I paused a moment to admire the high gilded ceiling, crystal chandeliers, and marble fireplace gracing the entry. Then, following the gold-lettered plaque, I hooked a right and headed for the bar. I reached the end of the hall, opened the door, and froze.

Clearly, this was what Gran had detected. I'd honestly never seen so many spirits gathered in one place. Dressed in finery from every era, entire generations continued hanging out at the club. The difficulty for a girl in my position lay in determining which of the people crammed in the small, wood paneled space were living, and which were dead. I sighted down the room and located Jackson sitting alone, hunched over the bar. He'd donned a sport coat over his jeans—in keeping with the requirement emblazoned on the front door—and his fingers clutched a tumbler of ice drowning in amber-colored liquid. I picked my way across the room and discovered trying to appear casual while zigzagging like a drunken monkey around people no one else can see is a challenge all its own. I made it to within six feet of the bar, when Darla popped up directly in front of me, and I skidded to a halt. Several revelers from both sides of the celestial divide favored me with curious looks.

"Do you mind?" I whispered through clenched teeth.

"Bunny Bartlett exiting the ladies' room. She's spotted Jackson and is approaching at three o'clock. This has been a Public Service Announcement. You're welcome."

I took a deep breath, squared my shoulders, and strode forward. I reached to tap Jackson on the shoulder. He turned, and then did a double take, just as a flash of fast moving blonde entered my peripheral vision, and slid onto the stool beside him.

"Lucy?" Jackson's eyes widened, then narrowed. He looked away. "What are you doing here?"

"We need to talk—" I began, but Bunny's unladylike snort that cut me off midsentence.

"Can't you take a hint, ghost girl? Now that he's satisfied his curiosity, Jackson is here. Where he belongs. Did you seriously think you could just sneak in and pass as someone who fits in?" She sneered. Then she offered Jackson a brilliant smile. "Don't fret, darling. I'll have security take care of this."

"Shut up, Bunny," Jackson snapped. He swiveled his stool toward me, showing her his back.

"Actually, Bunny." I flashed Harlan's guest pass. "I didn't sneak in. I walked right through the front door while the valet parked my car."

"How did you get that?" She gasped.

"Blackmail." I narrowed my eyes and glanced down at her feet resting on the bar rail. "Cute shoes. I bet you can barely wait for sandal season. As for passing as someone who fits in here, if that means someone like you, you couldn't pay me enough."

"Well, I never!" Bunny sputtered.

"I'm not the least bit surprised." I kept my tone level, struggling to ignore the curious dead who'd begun gathering around me, stroking my hair, and whispering my name, and focused my attention on Jackson. "As I said, we need to talk. I'd prefer to do it elsewhere. It's your call."

"I don't have anything else to say." Jackson picked up his glass and threw back a large slug of liquor. Bunny smirked, completely oblivious to the specter who sidled up and slid onto the barstool next to hers. He stared at me with dead, black, eyes and stroked Bunny's hair as though daring me to call him on it. Dude made my skin crawl. The whispers increased, swirling around me until I could barely hear my own thoughts, and more and more of the departed pressed in around me. I'd never experienced anything like it. Deadly cold seeped into my bones.

"Well, I have plenty," I insisted loudly. Perhaps the sound of my knees knocking together caught his attention, because Jackson finally deigned to glance my way. He shoved the glass from him, straightening in his seat. I must have looked as awful as I felt, because he slid from his barstool and reached for me. I took a step back.

"What's wrong?" His brows drew together.

"You need to get out, Lucy. I never would have let you come here if I'd realized sooner," Darla called frantically from the edge of the crowd. "There's too many. You can't handle them all."

"Look, I can't stay." I forced out through chattering teeth. "Please let me say this so I can leave. I put on this stupid dress, blackmailed Harlan out of his guest pass, and showed up here. To apologize. Somewhere along the way, it dawned on me I didn't have anything to apologize for. I'd given up hope of finding someone a long time ago. Then *you* pursued *me*. *You* brought gifts, *you* cooked dinner, *you* charmed the leopard print leggings off my grandmother, and *you* turned up the heat. Not that I was complaining. I even ignored common sense and past experience and stupidly allowed myself to believe. Then you snapped it off like a light switch, all but called me a slut and resorted to a pathetic cop-out like *it's not you, it's me*."

"Lucy, just calm down a minute—"

"Don't tell me to calm down! Never in the history of calming down has anyone ever calmed down by being told to calm down." Several people turned to stare. I ignored them, keeping my gaze firmly fixed on the cause of my ire. In fact, I had a pretty good head of steam going. Unfortunately, it did little to thaw the deep freeze rapidly enveloping me.

"You said *it was fun*," he frowned.

"I may not be a member of your exclusive society circle, and I don't follow convention, but I do have my pride. I'm used to slapping on a brave face." I shrugged. Oddly, my shoulders didn't actually move. "What did you expect me to say when you made it clear you'd changed your mind, or made a mistake, or…" I glared at Bunny. "Satisfied your curiosity?"

"You took it the wrong—"

"How should I have taken it? Believe me, I've heard that particular line before. You're right, Jackson. I'm not vanilla, and I don't want to be. I can't—won't—be anyone other than myself. Not anymore. Even if the price hurts. If that works for you, fine. If not, it's your prerogative. Either way, you should know you weren't alone in feeling something more. And that's all I came to say."

I dragged in a painful breath and turned away. Darla finally managed to elbow her way through the whispering throng to my side. She wrapped her arms around me, but I couldn't distinguish her touch from the pervasive cold consuming me. I gazed in terror at what appeared to be an army of phantoms standing between us and the door.

"I had no idea," Darla whispered against my ear. "They've been waiting years for someone to notice them. There's too many. You can't help them. You need to get out. Now."

"Lucy, wait!" Jackson's voice sounded faint and faraway, barely discernable over the escalating whispers filling my head. I gasped for air, concentrating on the exit, and used every ounce of strength I had to put one foot in front of the other. Darla, unable to physically help me, urged me on like a cheerleader on crack. My limbs refused to obey, the energy drain of so many spirits sucking at me like quicksand. Fortunately, Jackson's long fingers gripped my shoulders and spun me to face his annoyed expression.

"You can't just say your piece and walk…what the hell?" He caught me as I wrapped my fingers in the front of his jacket and my legs crumpled.

"P-P-Please," I whispered. "Get me out."

A collective sound rose from the Country Club set, gasps from living and groans from the dead, as Jackson hooked an arm beneath my knees. He swung me up against his chest—his wide, magnificent, and blessedly warm chest—and strode across the bar, down the hall, and through the vestibule.

"Sir, your jacket," the doorman shouted.

"Put it on my tab," Jackson called back. Ignoring the valet who jumped to his feet, he never broke stride as his long legs carried us across the parking lot. Darla streaked above us, a pale blur against the night sky in her agitated state. Finally, we reached Jackson's car, and he lowered me gently. He opened the door and helped me inside. Divesting himself of the sports coat, he draped it around my shoulders and jogged around to climb in the driver's side.

Jackson started the car and cranked on the heat. Trembling, I pulled my knees to my chest, gripped the edges of the jacket together with numb fingers, and burrowed into the lingering warmth from his body. Darla planted herself between us, careful not to touch me.

"Well, that was certainly a suckfest," Darla announced.

"Won't get any arguments from me," I whispered through stiff lips.

"No, I mean it literally," Darla continued in the most earnest voice I'd ever heard emerge from her pale lips. "I never realized it before, but you have a peculiar energy, Lucy. We—the dead, I mean—feed on it. I think it's connected to why you can see us. The amount of energy we channel from you is small, so when there's only a few of us around—like Grandpoppy and me—it doesn't seem to affect you. Scores of dead clamoring for attention all at once? They would've drained you dry. Suckfest. For the record, I forbid you to ever set foot in that place again."

"Come here." Jackson sighed in a voice dripping with exasperation. Perhaps assured of my momentary safety, or less likely, in observance of the ground rules, Darla looked back and forth between us, and then conveniently disappeared. I hesitated, but my discomfort trumped my pride. I scooted across the plush, leather seat. Jackson pulled me against him, wrapping his arms around me. Doubtless he would have done the same for anyone in my pathetic state, but I'd take what I could get at the moment, and snuggled into him.

"Better?" he asked when I finally stopped shivering. I nodded against his shoulder, loathe to extricate myself from the warm security of his embrace. "Good. Now, maybe you'd like to tell me exactly what just happened in there?"

"A Suckfest."

"What?"

"A Suckfest. Darla says ghosts feed off of my energy, and that's why I can see them. That place is crawling with spirits. So many in one place crying out to be heard drained me. Dangerously so. Apparently, the Douglasville Country Club needs a massive exorcism. Who knew?"

"Well, until it happens, you are not to cross the threshold again. I'll cancel our reservations for Saturday," Jackson said.

"You were planning to take me to the club? Where everyone would see us together?"

"Yes? Why wouldn't I? Now, maybe you'd like to explain exactly when I called you a slut."

"I didn't say you *called* me a slut. You implied it." Because it was entirely possible I stuck my lower lip out like a petulant two-year-old, I kept my face buried in the lapels of Jackson's sport coat.

"I did no such thing. I wanted you, you wanted me. Nothing wrong with it."

"Then why the sudden about face?"

"Look, I've had plenty of casual sex…" Jackson began.

"Thanks so much for sharing," I muttered. "Will we be approaching a station soon?"

"A station?"

"Yes, so I can disembark from this train of thought

187

before you regale me with the gory details of your previous carnal escapades." I glanced up at him through my lashes with a frown. He burst out laughing and squeezed me against him.

"I'm making a point, not a confession." He chuckled.

"And your point would be?"

"I'm not the man I was a week ago." Jackson shifted his position and looked directly into my eyes. "A week ago, I considered a couple of hours in the arms of a desirable woman simply a pleasant way to pass the time. Oh, all right, an *extremely* pleasant way to pass the time," he added when I skeptically raised my brows. "Then you plowed into me like a linebacker and changed all that."

"I see." He said he enjoyed *desirable* women. Then he compared me to a three hundred pound behemoth who flattens people for a living. Who wouldn't want a piece of that? I blinked back the hot tears threatening to escape, and shrugged his jacket from my shoulders. Then I leaned away from him to click off the heat before we both melted into puddles of glop. "I am deeply touched by your romantic sentiment. It's the first time anyone's given me credit for anything even remotely athletic."

Jackson let his arms fall away with a frown.

"Stop being deliberately obtuse. I spend half my time with corpses, so maybe I'm not very good at flowery speeches. Maybe my similes leave something to be desired. So, I'm just going to throw this out there like a cookie and hope the fact you came after me tonight means you're ready to bite. Until you, I was perfectly content with casual. I'll be damned if I know how it happened so quickly, but this thing between us isn't casual, Lucy. Not to me. Until you, I didn't believe in ghosts, never dreamed people wore stuffed animals on their feet, and thought love at first sight was a myth. When the truth smacked me in the head, I needed a minute to absorb it. So, I backed off. You took it as rejection and got defensive."

Which he then took as rejection. Maybe we should work on that. Wait. *Love at first sight?* My heart jumped in my chest, racing fast enough to run a thirty second mile. I cleared my throat. The voice that emerged still sounded two octaves deeper than usual.

"Of course people wear stuffed animals on their feet. How could you not know that? Were you raised in a bubble?" I mumbled.

"Yes. It's becoming more obvious to me every day." Jackson gathered me back into his arms and hooked a finger beneath my chin, forcing my eyes to his. They were dark, deep, and lit from within by a hint of laughter. "However, I think you're avoiding the subject."

"That's me. Totally skilled at deflecting deep emotional issues with my profound appreciation for cozy footwear. So, what do you think now?"

"Ghosts are people, too. There's something to be said for fuzzy footwear that stares back," he murmured, feathering soft kisses along my jaw. "And as for love at first sight—"

"Definitely not a myth." I gasped as Jackson's lips closed over mine in a kiss deep enough to drown me. I surrendered and took the plunge. As Darla can attest, there are worse ways to go.

Epilogue

One year later…

"I know you were leaning toward the zebra stripes and leather, but I think the blue is a good choice." Jackson pressed his lips to my cheek as his arms slipped around me from behind. The peaceful looking figure in the casket dressed in the conservative navy blue sheath dress and matching jacket, with rouge, lipstick, and presumably both upper and lower dentures intact, looked like *someone's* grandmother. Just not mine. Jackson would put her pearls and wedding rings on just before the guests were due to arrive. This ensured they wouldn't grow legs and walk off with one of the delivery people traipsing in and out of the parlor all day. It wasn't unheard of. Color me appalled.

"The *appropriate* choice, you mean," I sighed, turning to wrap my arms around him. "Well, my parents will approve, at any rate. They've never been big fans of anything other than vanilla."

"People do say it skips a generation. Just because they don't understand the joys of alternative flavors, doesn't mean they love you any less, Lucy. You do know that, right?"

"Yes, I know. Still, a girl can't help wishing they were a little more willing to embrace something that isn't a regular menu item." I propped my chin on his chest and looked into the loving eyes I'd come to know so well, wondering how I'd gotten so lucky. Then again, maybe luck had nothing to do with it. Gran said it had been destiny. "And don't think I didn't notice the tiara. Nice touch. She loved that tiara."

"Of course, she did. It was a gift from her favorite grandson-in-law." His arms tightened around me. "And just between us, her pink boa, motorcycle jacket, and rainbow disco wig are tucked in under the blanket at her feet."

"Thank you." I hugged him back. "At least she died wearing her red cowboy boots and gold bustier."

"That should make you happy."

"Well, it certainly made *Grandpoppy* happy." I snorted. "Though I think he was a little disappointed she forgot to put on the spurs that day."

"He'll get over it." Jackson laughed.

"I know Grandpoppy's been waiting to cross over for years, but I thought they'd stick around a while." I sighed, my heart aching as though someone held it in a tight fist. Even Mr. Picklepaw, who'd been strutting his three transparent testicles around Gran's ankles since choking to death on a hairball six months ago, had abandoned me to follow them into the afterlife. "I don't know what I'll do without them."

"Continue to love them, be grateful you had them in your life, and keep their memory alive in your heart. It's what the rest of the world does every day, and they don't have your absolute certainty the ones they love continue to live and love and be happy elsewhere. People die, Lucy. And they move on. It's the way it's supposed to be."

"I know." I nodded, throat tight. "And I have no

regrets, nothing left unsaid. It's just—"

"Hey, guess what!" Darla zipped through the wall of the elegant Victorian viewing parlor wearing a gleeful expression.

"*Most* people die and move on," I grumbled. "Some apparently didn't get the memo."

"Or figure it doesn't apply to them." My man-candy chuckled. "Darla?"

"Of course." I smirked. "Okay, I'll bite. What's your big news, Darla?"

"They've shut down the country club. Of course, the official story is they're closed for renovations. The truth is, they've had so many complaints from members regarding disturbing occurrences since the night you stormed in—and were carried out—they've decided to consult a medium to investigate. She is, of course, a complete fraud, but I suspect she'll have a few stories to tell."

"What kind of disturbing occurrences?"

"Well." Darla looked up at the ceiling and pasted on an innocent expression that didn't fool me for a second. "Among other things, Bunny Barlett's skirts developed this strange habit of flying up over her head. Usually in the middle of the dining room. She likes to go commando. Not pretty. It happened so often, she finally tried wearing slacks. Trust me, she did her fanny no favors. You're welcome."

"What do you mean, *you're welcome*?" I said, huffing out an exasperated breath.

"Well, I had to do *something*. All those deadbeats haunting the club were no help. Most of them just sit around pretending they aren't actually dead. If the medium confirms the place is haunted—which will be ensured by *moi*—they'll have to call in someone to exorcise the building. Once the departed depart, you and Jackson are free to patronize the place. Don't you see? The club is all about connections and networking. Haven't you noticed Jackson's had a lot more time on his hands over the past year? His competitors are taking advantage of his absence to steal the stiffs right out from under his nose!"

"Is that true?" I rounded on Jackson, eyes narrowed, arms akimbo.

"Is what true?" He grinned. "I can't hear her, remember?"

"You've stopped going to the club because of me, and your business is suffering for it?"

"I've no desire to go if you aren't with me. Yeah, business *has* dropped off a bit, but we're hardly in dire straits. Everybody dies. We aren't likely to become obsolete. Besides, I can afford to throw the other guys a bone. Between my inheritance, my savings, and my investments, we could both retire quite comfortably tomorrow." His wide, magnificent shoulders rose and fell.

"Jackson," I whispered in a strangled voice as his implication struck home. I'd never asked. It never seemed important. I loved the man, not the money. "Exactly how much money do we have?"

"Lots." A wide grin split his face.

"Lots," I repeated absently. Should I offer to sign a pre-nup? How did that work if you were already married? I'd have to check into it. I coughed and turned back to Darla. "See, we're fine. We appreciate your thoughtfulness, but you should probably stop exposing Bunny's girly bits to all and sundry. Probably."

"I can still hide her pumps so she's forced to wear sandals, right?"

"No."

"How about food coloring in her shampoo?"

"Absolutely not." I pictured Bunny's platinum mane streaked with a rich shade of green and bit my lip to keep from smiling. That one actually had potential.

"Well, what if I—"

"Darla…" I drawled in a warning tone. The doorbell chimed, announcing the arrival of yet another tasteful bouquet.

"Duty calls," Jackson pressed his lips to mine and headed for the door. The flowers, cards, and memorial donations to Bikers Without Wheels poured in. I swallowed hard. Despite her eccentricities, people in this town apparently recognized what I'd always known. Beneath her leather and tassels, my gran was a truly amazing lady.

"Peanut Butter Fudge, Lucy. You suck all the life out of death. *You* are going to be the most boring ghost *ever*," she sniffed. "Fortunately, you'll have me to show you the ropes."

"Well, I'm not planning on becoming a ghost anytime soon. You may have to wait around a while," I laughed.

"Not a problem," she announced airily. "I have no intention of following your grandparents' example in the foreseeable future. I cannot possibly leave this world until I figure out a way to divest Harlan of his orange and green plaid polyester golf pants. I mean, we *are* still married. No woman in her right mind would risk having to look upon them for all eternity should Harlan have the bad luck—or poor taste—to die while wearing them. In case you were worried."

"I wasn't." Truthfully, I'd grown so used to having Darla Swithers around, I sometimes forgot she was dead. "I thought you succeeded in dousing them in red wine?"

"An exercise in futility. Who knew the son-of-a beechnut-tree had an entire drawer filled with back-ups?" She groused, drifting over to the casket. "Jackson did a marvelous job. It looks lovely."

"I think you mean *she*," I said, moving to stand beside her. I gripped the edge of the casket until my knuckles blanched, and gazed down at the woman who'd been mother, father, and everything in between for so much of my life. I wondered if anyone would ever love me so unconditionally again. Her absence left a hole in my heart the size of Texas.

"No, I mean *it*. Think about it, Lucy. This isn't Gran. The body is a pot. It contained a beautiful plant. It nurtured the plant, and protected it, and kept it safe for a very long time. But it was never designed to contain the plant beyond a certain point. The pot grew old and cracked and worn, suffocating the roots, stifling the plant and keeping it from growing. Only by being transplanted could the plant continue to thrive and bloom. Gran is the plant and now she's found a fertile field and is bursting with flowers. This is just the pot."

I swiveled my head in Darla's direction, and my mouth dropped open. There are moments in life which leave an indelible imprint on your brain. Or a permanent scar, as the case may be. You know the ones I mean. The first time the man of your dreams said 'I love you.' Your wedding day. The day you realized the girl who tormented you in high school somehow became your best friend. Though she's dead as a doornail. I'd been as guilty as Darla of judging a book by its cover. Apparently, even a self-absorbed adolescent socialite who failed study hall can grow into a woman who exhibits moments of profundity. I closed my eyes and pictured Gran in a bright meadow, face upturned to the sun, happy and blooming. Although, let's face it, Gran, in her inimitable individuality, would probably be a big, honking hydrangea bush, or maybe a rhododendron, in the field of daisies and buttercups.

"Thank you, Darla. Oddly, that actually makes me feel better."

"Good." Dara smiled. "Then my work here is done. Now, if you'll excuse me, I need to see a man about some pants." She faded out, dissipating just as Jackson placed the newly arrived arrangement on a side table and stepped over to slip his arms around my waist. He pulled me back against him. I relaxed my body along the length of his, grateful for his strength, his unwavering love, his total acceptance of all I am no matter what the Douglasville Debs, or anyone else thinks. And that's when it hit me. I stiffened.

"You okay?" He pressed his lips to the top of my head.

I stepped free of his embrace and slipped a hand beneath the satin blanket he'd neatly folded over Gran's feet, tugging her pink, feather boa free. I peeked at him over my shoulder and grinned.

"I will be. Could you give me a hand?"

Jackson never questioned it. He simply helped me artfully loop and drape the gaudy accessory, and we stepped back to admire our handiwork. Have I mentioned how much I love this guy?

"What changed your mind?" Jackson asked, looping an arm around my shoulders to pull me close.

"You."

"Me?" He elevated his brows in surprise. "What did I do?"

"Eventually, we all reach the end of our road together in this life. When we do, we leave behind the cars, the country club membership, the designer duds. None of those things matter. Gran wasn't a conservative blue silk dress. She was a pink feather boa and a shiny tiara. I'm okay with that. And anyone who isn't? They didn't know her, let alone appreciate her. Screw them."

"Screw them," my hunka-hunka burning love agreed, capturing my lips in a slow, gentle kiss. He raised his head, and his eyes reflected the smoldering passion that still made my girly bits quiver...every time.

"And what did you do?" I repeated his question back to him. "You were a man with a certain position—status, shall we say—in this town. Yet, you didn't judge her. You didn't judge me. You bought me elephant slippers. You helped me understand the important thing is who we are inside, how we live, and how we treat others. You show me every day what matters most is what we mean to those who mean the most to us. You never asked me to be anything other than who and what I am. You helped me believe in myself, because you believed in me. You accepted me, and loved me, and didn't give a flying fig what anyone else thought."

"And I never will. Well, unless the Douglasville Debs start showing up at the door asking for séances and palm readings. Mother's heard rumors." His grin widened almost as much as my eyes.

"They wouldn't!"

"They might." He shrugged.

"Assuming I was agreeable, and let's be clear, *I am not*. It doesn't work that way. At least not in my case."

"Well, it could, dear," came a loving and familiar voice I never expected to hear. Hot tears sprang reflexively to my eyes. "It's probably best to keep that to yourself. Oh, look, Eugene. Jackson remembered my tiara. And Lucy broke down and added the boa. Thank you, dear. I'd lobby for the leather, but I suspect it would set your mother off, and hysteria is so unbecoming at these functions."

"Gran?" I whispered, my eyes darting around the parlor, heart racing. "I don't see you. Where are you?"

"In your heart, dear. Right where I'll always be."

"Gran?" Jackson's eyes widened and gleamed with moisture. He'd loved her, too. He'd fully embraced both our brands of crazy. Who could resist such a man? Not this girl. And, unbelievably, he was all mine. I squeezed his trim waist, and his arms tightened around me. "But, how—"

"I have no idea." I shook my head. "She said she and Grandpoppy were crossing over."

"Oh, we did, dear." Gran's giggle echoed through the parlor. "Whatever made you think the road to ever-after was a one way street?"

A word about the author…

Sharon Saracino was born and raised in beautiful Northeastern Pennsylvania. Always the girl with her nose in a book, a lifelong love of writing took a back seat to real life while she got married, raised a family, and finally decided what she wanted to be when she grew up! She frequently announced that someday she was going to write a book. One milestone birthday (we won't discuss which one!) she decided someday would be here and gone if she didn't get her butt in gear. She plans to win the lottery just as soon as she remembers to purchase a ticket, fantasizes about moving to Italy, brews limoncello, adores her family, and believes there's always magic to be found if you only take the time to look for it!

http://sharonsaracino.com

www.ingramcontent.com/pod-product-compliance
Lightning Source LLC
Chambersburg PA
CBHW060929180626
46817CB00004B/1462